THE FORBIDDEN TREASURE

Cosette, Cillian, & Nathan Willard

The Forbidden Treasure
A Mystery Lake Adventure

Written and Illustrated

by

Cosette, Cillian, & Nathan Willard

Cover Art

by

Paul Guinan

Arbroath Publishing   2021

The Forbidden Treasure: A Mystery Lake Adventure
Text and Pictures Copyright © 2021 by
Nathan Willard, Cosette Willard, and Cillian Willard

All rights reserved.
No part of this this book may be used or reproduced in any manner whatsoever without written permission, except for review purposes.

This is a work of fiction.

Arbroath Publishing, LLC
www.arbroathpublishing.com
www.mysterylakeadventure.com

ISBN 978-1-7371504-9-7 (paperback)
ISBN 978-1-7371504-5-9 (e-book)

FIRST EDITION

In Loving Memory of
Dan and Mary

Contents

The Discovery 1

The Town of Little Mystery Lake 11

Jax Spreads the News 21

The Club 33

A Mystery Revealed 45

Alistair McQueen 55

Back Again 69

Nunquam Non Paratus 83

The Heist 93

Stuck in the Past 103

The Confrontation 111

What Now? 119

Things Do Not Go as Planned 129

~ Chapter 1 ~

The Discovery

The first day of school can be the best experience of your life.

You finally get to see your friends again after a couple month break, and tell them about all the adventures you had last summer. You get to see who your new teacher is, hopefully one who likes you. You get new clothes, a new desk, a new locker, new art supplies—there are so many exciting new things to explore.

But it can also be a terrifying experience—especially if it's the first day at a new school, and you just moved into your new neighborhood, into a place far from your old hometown, and you hardly know a single person in this new place.

That's what this first day of school was like for Alice and her twin brother Jax.

Still, Alice was determined to impress her new teacher. She didn't care so much about what her classmates thought—they probably wouldn't enjoy her company anyway—and she didn't think she'd have much in common with most of them. But she sure wanted her teacher to admire her.

As for Jax, he was attempting to hide from the bully who had chased him into the school auditorium.

"Hey, where'd you go?" the bully called out.

Jax hid behind some stage props, trying not to move an inch, trying his hardest to be silent. But his heart was pounding, and his lungs desperately wanted to suck in deep, long, *loud* breaths. But he didn't dare; he fought against the burning in his lungs, and held his breath as long as he could.

"I just want to talk to you," the bully said. "I'm a nice guy. We can be friends. My name's Zach."

Zach slowly made his way through the auditorium, checking every single row.

A folding chair got in Zach's way, and with a kick he sent it clanging across the slick linoleum floor.

Jax's heart started beating faster. He didn't dare imagine what Zach might do to him. But he had to breathe.

No, he'll hear me. But before Jax had a chance to stop himself, he had sucked in a deep, loud breath. He

The Forbidden Treasure

quickly clasped his hands over his mouth, desperately trying to silence his breathing.

Zach's eyes darted towards the stage. His smile was sinister. If Jax could have seen it, he'd know exactly what the expression on Zach's face meant: *I've got you now.*

Zach stepped up onto the stage just as Alice pushed open the door to the auditorium, stopping Zach in his tracks.

"Jax," she cried out with a concerned voice. "Where are you?"

Zach spun around to face her. "What do you want?" he demanded fiercely.

Alice eyed Zach suspiciously. "Jax, ARE YOU IN HERE?!" she shouted.

"There's no one in here except me," Zach lied, with a grin on his face.

"Why are you here?" Alice asked. "Why are the lights off?"

But before Zach answered, Jen entered the auditorium. "I'm sick of looking for your stupid brother," she said.

* * * *

Alice had been sat next to Jen in class.

Ms. Zeldin, their teacher, was constantly complimenting Jen. She'd say, "For later reference, class, use Jen's work as an example," or "Look at how neat Jen's handwriting is. I sure wish that I could read everyone else's as easily as hers."

Ms. Zeldin had not given Alice one compliment yet. So Alice wasn't very thrilled when their teacher gave Jen the opportunity to show Jax and her around the school.

Ms. Zeldin thought Alice would like this since Jen actually knew Alice. Jen's family had moved to Mystery Lake from California about a year ago. And Jen had actually lived in the same neighborhood in San Francisco as Alice, before she moved.

Alice tried to convince Ms. Zeldin they didn't need a guide to get them around the school. They could find their way around by themselves. But Ms. Zeldin insisted.

"If we don't get back to class soon," warned Jen, "Ms. Zeldin will blame me. Even though it's your dumb brother's fault…" She stopped. She stared at Zach. A lump stuck in her throat.

"Jax," Alice called out, "please come out!"

Jax was about to call back, then stopped. He knew Alice couldn't protect him from this bully. And if he dared to call out, then Alice was going to have the bully after her too.

"I'm leaving and going back to class. Go find your stupid brother yourself," Jen said.

"Why should I care? Just go! It's not like I'm the stupid one!" Alice shouted back.

"You need to come with me. *Now*," Jen demanded.

"Never in a million years would I come with you," Alice said stubbornly.

"I'll take care of her," offered Zach. "I can help her."

This didn't sound like a very good idea to Alice. Between Jen and Zach, she'd much rather be stuck with Jen.

"You didn't even see what happened to him," Jen said. "He probably just wandered back to class on his own."

Jax wouldn't do that, Alice thought. *It isn't like him to just leave me without saying anything. But maybe so.* She was upset with him for abandoning her. *He probably made some new friends on the playground and forgot all about me. In that case he can take care of himself.*

The auditorium door shut behind the girls, and Zach turned back to the stage. Now that those girls were gone, he could get back to finding that little twerp. He didn't know exactly how he'd deal with Jax when he found him. Maybe he'd pin him down and thump him in the chest until Jax went nuts and begged for mercy. Maybe he'd stuff him in a trash can, and then roll it down the hall and get some of his friends to join in on the fun. Or maybe he'd just punch him in the face.

It didn't really matter to him what he ended up doing. He was just looking forward to messing Jax up.

"Come on, Jax," Zach coaxed, "come out and play." Zach pulled back the stage curtain. He peered into the shadows, letting his eyes adjust, searching the darkness for Jax's hiding place.

Jax had to make another plan. He could sense Zach getting closer. He couldn't keep hiding much longer.

Jax sprung from his hiding place, and sprinted for the exit, stage right.

Zach lumbered after him.

Zach was nearly on him now. He reached out and grabbed Jax's shirt. But in a fit of wild panic, Jax wriggled free.

Jax pulled a podium down as he ran. Zach smashed into it—shin first. Zach crashed to the ground, falling hard, and slid into a backdrop that fell down on top of him.

Jax burst through the stage door and didn't look back. But he could hear Zach thrashing around and yelling as he tried to untangle himself.

Jax ran down the hall, looking for somewhere to hide where Zach would never find him.

He ran and ran, pulling on doors, trying to find one that was unlocked.

The Forbidden Treasure

Finally, one door swung open, into what looked like an old storage room, probably for a science class. There were old beakers and test tubes, Bunsen burners, specimen jars—some of them filled with weird dead animals preserved in formaldehyde.

Jax wasn't in the Mystery Lake Elementary school anymore. He had stumbled into the high school, which was attached to their school building.

He crept through the storage room, trying not to look at the dead animals that stared at him from their jars with dead eyes. In a different light he would have found them interesting, but he wasn't happy about being stuck with them in a dimly lit storage room. He just needed to find a small nook to hide in.

He was poking around the back of the room, trying not to break anything, when he came across something very strange. Maybe it was the light playing tricks on his eyes, but it looked like it belonged in a science-fiction movie. It was like a giant metal egg, covered in buttons and crisscrossed with wires. And then there was a hose coming out of it, with a nozzle, like what you'd see at a gas station for pumping gas. What could that possibly be for?

He stood there, wondering what this machine was.

Someone opened the storage room door and flipped on the light.

Jax scooted over beside a bookcase and tried to hide himself.

"Who's there?" a man called out. "No one is supposed to be in this room."

The man cautiously walked to the back of the room. He reached the machine, picked up a large tarp from the ground beside it and threw it over the top. He smoothed down the tarp, till he was sure the machine was completely covered.

Jax shifted to a different hiding place, trying to shrink back even further. But his foot kicked a rolling cart, and a beaker tipped and fell, smashing on the floor.

The man spun around.

The Forbidden Treasure

Willard

~ Chapter 2 ~

The Town of Little Mystery Lake

Alice trudged slowly down the sidewalk, alone and angry.

Jax hadn't come back to class. *Where would he have gone?* She did not know. Her class had been dismissed and the school day was over, and now, she was walking home alone.

Jen walked about fifty yards ahead, talking and laughing with a friend. You see, even though they had known each other before, and their parents enjoyed each other's company, Jen did not count Alice as her friend. Really, Jen and Alice did not care for each other at all.

Alice could remember when she heard the news Jen's family was moving. She had felt only the slightest bit sorry for Jen, and she really wasn't that sad to see her go. They hadn't always got along. And they had very different interests—Jen always insisted on playing with dolls, but Alice didn't care for dolls anymore; she would rather jump off a bridge.

Alice felt a little sorry for Jen, because she thought if she had to move to Oregon it would be terrible. She had known Jen for so long, and she did care about her. Still, she didn't want to live near her for a second time.

But now they were living next door to each other again. Jen hadn't come over to visit when they moved in. Alice saw her peeking out her window—watching them standing in their new front yard as the movers carried in the furniture. She knew Jen was spying on her and Jax as they played in their backyard. And now Jen only paid attention to her at school because Ms. Zeldin forced her to.

I hate this town, Alice thought bitterly.

Alice was ten years old, so was Jax. As I mentioned earlier, they were twins—fraternal twins, which means not identical. But you probably already know a boy and a girl can't possibly be identical twins. They were both extraordinarily brave children, and sought adventure more than just about anything. But now they had just been moved to the town of Mystery Lake, Oregon, which was a very old, very boring-looking town, as far as Alice was concerned.

Mystery Lake had only three schools: Mystery Lake Elementary, Junior High, and the High School. The town had a few rundown buildings on its one main street, a cafe, a few stores, and a couple of rusty old parks.

It was famous (if you could say that) for an enormous lake that stretched on for miles: Mystery Lake. The city of Eugene wasn't too far away. That's where the University of Oregon was, where their mom had just recently been hired to work at the research lab. So maybe there was exploring to be done there, and some adventures to be had. Still, it couldn't possibly be as fun as sailing in the bay, hiking through the redwoods, or climbing Mt. Tamalpais.

Why here? thought Alice.

As Alice trudged slowly down the sidewalk, she thought back to the moment when she found out her family was leaving San Francisco—*July 15.*

Without any warning, their parents sat them down and told them they had to move. Their mom had some new and important job. They had already found a home, all thanks to Jen's parents. And they'd be living near their dad's brother Tony, who was a science teacher at Mystery Lake High School.

Alice and Jax had walked slowly to the table, sensing that something must be wrong. Alice had prayed that her parents were not going to say those three words that would change her life forever. Alice and Jax loved San Francisco as much as they loved their parents (well, maybe not as much, but close). But their mom did say the words, the three awful words: *We are moving.*

"Dad and I have talked about this for years and have finally decided to move to Oregon. We will not argue. We are moving in a month. We will not tolerate complaining. We have already bought the house. We just need to get this house looking nice. What's done is done. We know you love San Francisco, but it will be good to have you try something else for a change."

Alice tried to hold back her tears. Tears of anger. *Please be a dream!* Alice pleaded with herself.

Jax slumped down in his chair and scowled.

That night at dinner, she didn't eat a thing. Why had their parents been so mean? She did not know, but she would never forgive them.

Alice pushed open the front door to her new house and threw her bag to the ground.

"Dad?" she called out. "Where were you? *Dad!* I thought you were going to meet me after school. Jax left without me."

The Forbidden Treasure

"I'm so sorry." Alice's dad stepped out of the kitchen into the living room. "I should have met you. I lost track of time."

Uncle Tony stepped out beside him.

"I was talking with your uncle. He brought Jax home early. He found Jax hiding in his lab, but Jax wouldn't tell Uncle Tony why. Do you know what happened?"

"No," said Alice. "He just disappeared at afternoon recess. I tried to find him, but I have no idea what he was doing."

"I think he was running from someone," said Uncle Tony.

"I don't know," Alice replied. "There are so many creeps and jerks at that stupid school. Who knows?"

"Alice," said her dad.

"What? I hate it. I wish we never moved here."

"Well, we did. So you're going to have to get used to it."

"Get used to having no friends, and living in the most boring town in the whole world?"

"Alice," said Uncle Tony, "I think if you give it a chance, you'll find Mystery Lake is a pretty great place."

"I don't see that happening."

"Not with a horrible attitude like that," said her dad.

"I…" Alice tried to reply, but her dad interrupted her.

"I'm not going to argue with you. And you're being rude to your uncle. Get upstairs to your room."

Alice glared at her dad, but didn't say a word. She stomped up the stairs to her room and slammed the door.

Alice took a deep breath and sighed. She may have hated Mystery Lake, but she did like her new room. It had a big bay window that looked out over the front yard, and across the street stood the spookiest-looking house Alice had ever seen. To her, that was a good thing. She was the type of girl who loved cats, particularly black cats. She had named her black cat Doom.

The house must have been at least a hundred years old. It was built in the Gothic style. (Alice didn't know this, but she would have loved that word—gothic.) Whoever had built it must have really wanted a castle, but had to make do with a house. They may have still gotten a dungeon. Or perhaps the tower, which loomed over the structure, contained a small cell at the top to lock a prisoner away.

It looked straight out of a horror movie—decaying and abandoned, its windows and doors boarded up—and certainly full of mystery. Alice couldn't wait to find a way in; she was certain there would be some forgotten treasure somewhere inside.

As she was lost in her imagination, dreaming of what she might discover, her fingers busied themselves by running over the well-worn wood of the bench seat that was permanently fixed below the bay window. They found a raised seam in the paneling below the window. With a little tug, a piece of the wood came loose and clattered on the bench.

Alice was startled out of her fantasy. "Oh no," she whispered. Her dad was not going to be happy about that. Maybe she could just stick it back on and her dad would never notice.

Alice picked the piece of wood up. There were no nails in it. *How was it supposed to stick in place?* Alice thought.

As she looked at it and the spot it came from, she realized it must be meant to be removed, hiding a secret compartment. Alice slid it into place, flush with the rest of the trim, just as it should be. Then using her fingernail to pry at the seam, she was able to pull it loose again.

Removing the piece of wood revealed a hole someone had made in the wall. She peered into the opening, but couldn't really see anything. She needed light.

Alice grabbed a jewelry box off the bookcase next to her. There was a little mirror on the lid. She opened the box and tried to reflect some light into the hole.

What was that? A little glint of something shiny and green. She needed a flashlight. *Where did dad put them?*

A car pulled into the driveway below. Alice looked up; her mom was home. She quickly returned the piece of wood to its place; she didn't want anyone else discovering her secret before she had a chance to properly inspect the contents. But it would have to wait.

She quickly ran downstairs. Feeling bad about her outburst at her dad earlier, she wanted to get on the good side of her mom before her dad might tell her what Alice did and get her in trouble. She didn't want to lose her chance to stay up late reading that night, and she was really wanting to finish the next chapter in the book she had been reading for two days.

Alice ran down the stairs, nearly falling, and jumped up onto her mom just as she entered the front door.

"I love you," said Alice.

"Woah," her mom exclaimed, bracing herself against the door. "I love you too. Let me put my stuff down. You're going to knock me over."

Alice didn't want to let go.

"Did you have a good day?" she asked as Alice's dad entered the room.

Alice glanced at her dad, afraid of how he thought the day had gone.

"Go back upstairs," her dad said.

"No. May I please talk to mom?"

"Go." Her dad pointed towards her room.

Alice hesitated.

The Forbidden Treasure

"What's wrong?" her mom asked, as she set down her bags. "Did Alice do something?"

"No, it's Jax," her dad responded.

Alice was relieved. *Too bad for Jax, but at least she wasn't in trouble. And besides, he deserved it for abandoning her at lunch.*

Willard

~ Chapter 3 ~

Jax Spreads the News

That night in bed, Alice lay under her covers—motionless, wide awake, eyes on the ceiling. Her mind was whirring, filled with worries and hopes fighting for attention.

Alice made up her mind that she couldn't stand Mystery Lake, Ms. Zeldin her teacher, and pretty much everyone that lived in this town.

Lost in her thinking, she didn't hear Jax sneak into her room and tip-toe up to her bed.

So she jumped when he whispered, "Pssst.".

"Jax!" she whisper-yelled, her heart thumping hard from the fright.

"Quiet," Jax scolded, covering her mouth. He stopped to listen, making sure his parents hadn't heard, fearing at any moment his dad would march up the stairs, throw the door open, and put him right back in his bed.

Jax hadn't been able to sleep either, worried that he saw something in his uncle's lab that he shouldn't have seen.

"Uncle Tony has a time machine in his lab," Jax said, trying really hard to make sure he didn't sound like an idiot.

Alice calmly pushed her brother's hand from her mouth. "Jax, that is the stupidest thing you've ever said." She sighed. "And you've said some pretty stupid…"

"I'm serious," Jax interrupted. "I'm sure of it. Whatever it is, I really want to try it out." "Well, you better not, because he won't be happy to find us sneaking around his storage room again!" Alice whispered sternly.

"When did that stop you?" Jax responded. "You know you're not supposed to go in that house across the street, but you know you're going to try."

"Yeah, but that's an abandoned house." said Alice. "You want to sneak into our uncle's lab. He's already caught you once. What do you think mom and dad will do to us if they find out we've broken into Uncle Tony's lab again and are messing around with his stuff?"

"We won't get caught," Jax assured her.

"So we're going to travel through time, with his time machine, and no one will find out?" said Alice. "Have you lost your mind?!"

"If we get caught, we'll sneak back later and go back in time and keep ourselves from getting caught," said Jax.

"It's *not* a time machine!" Alice replied through gritted teeth.

"It *is*," said Jax.

"How would you know that?" asked Alice.

"The internet," said Jax. "I did some googling of our uncle. There's all sorts of stuff on him. Know what I found?"

"Did he publish a How to Make a Time Machine manual? That would be a pretty good clue," said Alice.

"No, but he has given some talks about time travel," Jax snapped. "I found a video of him speaking at some college. Most people just think he's crazy. But after seeing that machine, I don't know what else it could be."

"Maybe it's just a pile of junk," said Alice.

"Would it hurt to find out?" Jax asked.

Alice stopped disagreeing with her brother long enough to think for a moment. Maybe Mystery Lake wasn't going to be as boring as she thought after all.

Her mom was a pretty important scientist, from what she heard her talking to her dad about. Maybe the reason why they came to Oregon was because of her uncle. Maybe her parents weren't just trying to be mean. Maybe her uncle needed her mom's help. Maybe that's why her uncle went out of his way to bring Jax home early and talk to dad about what Jax saw. He probably wanted to make sure Jax didn't get too curious. He wanted to make sure they stayed out of the way. Well, she was more than curious: she was suspicious. *What were they hiding?*

"Ok," she said, "but if anything goes wrong, I'm blaming it all on you."

* * * *

The next morning was only their second day of school. If that machine wasn't a time machine, or something interesting, this year was going to be really long and really boring. Alice sat up straight at her desk. She checked the clock. She couldn't wait. The minutes were dragging by.

Alice checked the clock for about the 100th time. Finally! It was time for lunch.

In the cafeteria she took a seat at the same table as Jen. Alice opened her lunch box. A peanut butter and honey sandwich, and some pretzels; not exciting, but she was certain it was better than the hot lunch. The smell of the cafeteria food made her gag.

Jen glared at Alice.

Katie, Jen's friend, whispered into Jen's ear. Jen's eyes became slits as she shot Alice her most ferocious glare. She got up, moved to another table. Katie and the rest of her friends followed.

Fine, Alice thought, *I'm trying to be your friend, but if you don't want to be my friend, I don't care.*

Alice was startled out of her brooding as Jax plopped down beside her.

"We don't have time to eat," Jax said.

"What?" said Alice.

"I'm not waiting till after school," said Jax.

"We've got 45 minutes. Let's go now."

"Now?"

"Yeah, there's going to be a lot more kids walking around—nobody will pay attention to us."

Alice threw her sandwich back in her lunch box and jumped up from the table.

They rushed out of the cafeteria, down the hallway towards Uncle Tony's storage room.

Their eagerness did not go unnoticed. *Where are they running?* thought Jen. She was going to find out. "Stay here," she told her friends as she got up from the lunch table and followed the twins.

Jax and Alice stood in front of the machine. Jax pulled back the tarp. He slowly stepped into it, and Alice followed.

There must be thousands of tiny buttons, switches and lights on this machine, thought Jax. "Which ones do we push?"

"I don't know," said Alice.

Jax inspected the control board. It looked like there were two main knobs. When you turned them, they lit up a digital screen. The first knob simply switched to + or - . The second made numbers appear, like on a digital clock. So, if this *was* a time machine, he figured there must be one knob to tell the machine if you wanted to go back or forward in time, and one that told the machine how much time to go back or forward.

They turned the first knob back to minus. They turned the second knob one click to .000001. That couldn't be much time, so they turned it to -64.

"Now what?" asked Alice.

A button in the middle of the board lit up green. Jax pushed it.

There was a sudden flash of light, and a loud bang.

Alice pushed back the tarp. Everything looked different. They were no longer in the storage room; they were in the middle of a jungle. It reminded Alice of the Jurassic Park movies.

Jax pushed past Alice, stepping out of the time machine. "Holy crap it worked! It really worked. I can't believe it! This is amazing."

Alice was silent, stunned, her eyes as round saucers. *It really had worked.*

"Look at the size of this thing." Jax was holding a leaf the size of two elephant's ears.

"Where are we?!" he exclaimed.

"I think we probably should have used a smaller number," said Alice.

"How far do you think we went back?" Jax asked.

"I have no idea," said Alice.

"This is so cool," said Jax. "Let's find out." He pushed the large plants out of his way and began to walk into the jungle.

Alice didn't move.

Jax turned back to her. "Come on. You don't need to be afraid."

"You don't know that," said Alice. She took a deep breath, then followed.

Other than some ridiculously large plants and a frighteningly large dragonfly—which thankfully quickly flew a way and took no interest in the twins—they didn't find much. As they walked further and further away from the time machine, they just found more jungle.

"Maybe it just took us to South America or something," suggested Alice. She turned around looking back along their path, making sure they didn't lose their way back to the time machine.

"This doesn't just look like some jungle in South America. I think…"

Jax froze.

"What?" asked Alice. She turned towards Jax and ran into his back. "Jax…"

"Quiet!"

Alice looked past Jax. There in front of them was a sleeping tyrannosaurus rex.

With their bodies jittering from the adrenaline rush that had instantly shot through them, as cautiously as they could they turned back towards the time machine, and as quickly but as silently as possible, they ran.

Where is that stupid machine?! Alice frantically thought. *We should have been back to it by now. Did we get lost? No, we couldn't have. I broke branches off the plants as we went, marking the path. This is the way we came. We hadn't walked this far, had we?*

There was a large crash behind them, "Uh, Jax we should probably hurry."

"I AM HURRYING!"

Large booming footsteps filled the jungle. Slow at first, but then quicker, and quicker, quicker—it was running.

"*GO!*" yelled Alice.

Jax didn't need to be told. He was already sprinting.

Finally—there was the time machine. Jax jumped inside. "Come on!"

The Forbidden Treasure

Alice stepped in a large mud puddle, which sucked her shoe off as she tried to pull her foot out and brought her crashing to the ground.

She struggled to get back to her feet...

A deafening screech echoed across the mountains.

Alice looked up. There above the trees was the head of the T-Rex looking down at her.

"Get up!" Jax grabbed her by the arm, dragging her onto her feet and into the time machine.

Alice couldn't take her eyes off the beast. "*Jax!*" she screamed.

The monster pushed through the jungle, crashing through the trees, its thundering footsteps crushing everything beneath them, splinters flying. It was staring right at her—its head tilted to the side like a bird, intently focused on her as it ran straight towards them.

Alice closed her eyes.

There was a loud bang.

Alice opened her eyes. Same old closet. Same old creepy pictures of presidents. Same old everything. They were back home.

"*Woah*," Jax said, gasping for breath. "That was crazy! Oh man, it works. I told you. I can't believe it. This is so awesome. I told you it was a time machine."

"We can't use it," said Alice.

"Can't use it, are you crazy?"

"It's too dangerous."

"We just need to be careful, not go back so far."

Alice grabbed Jax by the shoulders and yelled in his face, "We almost died!"

"But we didn't," said Jax, smirking. "This is the most amazing thing that has ever happened to us, and now you get chicken. We have to use it again."

"Use what again?" asked Jen.

The Forbidden Treasure

~ Chapter 4 ~

The Club

"Why so quiet?" asked their dad, as he spooned another helping of green beans onto his plate.

Alice had barely touched her dinner. And the normally talkative Jax hadn't said more than three words. They were guilty, and they knew it. At any moment Uncle Tony would probably burst in the front door and drag them off to jail, or worse.

What was worse than jail? They didn't know, and that's what was so frightening about it.

Alice glared at her parents. *It was all their fault. This would have never happened if they hadn't moved.*

Jax had wanted to tell Jen. But Alice refused. *If we had told her what had happened, there's no way she would have believed us, and for sure she would have just gone and tattled on us. And then the teacher would tell our parents.*

No, we couldn't tell Jen. She would get us into even more trouble. She was probably going to tell on us for sneaking into the storage room without permission.

Alice had expected Jen to run off and tell Ms. Zeldin right then. But for some reason she didn't. Instead Jen just looked at the time machine over, inspecting all its parts.

"What does it do?" Jen asked.

Jax said, "It's a…"

"We don't know," Alice said, interrupting Jax and elbowing him in the side.

"Really?" Jen responded. "If you don't know what it does, then what was that flash of light and loud bang?"

"I don't know what you're talking about," said Alice.

"Did you hear that loud bang, Jax?" Jen asked.

Jax hesitated. "Uhh." He looked at Alice.

The death stare she was giving him obviously meant *don't say anything.*

"Uh, no," Jax replied.

Jen looked Jax straight in the eyes—he looked down at his feet. She shifted her gaze to Alice—Alice did not look away. For an uncomfortable moment they glared at each other.

"I'm going to find out what's going on," said Jen.

"We don't know what you're talking about. There's nothing to find out," said Alice. "We just wanted to talk to our uncle; we thought he'd be here."

"They must be doing some science experiments at the high school," said Jax. "That must be what you heard."

Jen looked Jax and Alice up and down. "Why are you covered in mud?" she asked. "And what happened to your shoe?"

* * * *

Alice grabbed her plate and scrambled up from the kitchen table. Jax shoved one more bite in his mouth and followed.

"Just where do you think you're going without being excused first?" their dad demanded. "Ummm, to do my homework," Alice replied, then gave him her biggest smile. *There, that should convince him.*

They didn't have homework, and Alice couldn't imagine what type of boring homework Ms. Zeldin would give them in the following week. Probably something to do with geometry. Alice hated geometry, but she couldn't think about that right now. They had bigger problems on their hands.

"I don't think so. Come back here, now," their mom said, and gave them a look. "You don't have any homework, Alice Whitmer."

"Sit down and talk to us," their dad said.

Reluctantly, Jax and Alice sat back down.

"What do you want to talk about?" asked Jax.

"Tell us about your day," said their mom. "What did you do?"

"Just went to school," said Alice. "What do you think? Just the same boring thing as the day before."

"It better not have been the same as yesterday," said their dad. "I sure hope you weren't pestering your uncle again."

"I wasn't pestering him," said Jax.

"We know you like Uncle Tony," said their mom. "But he has classes he needs to attend to."

"I just got lost," said Jax.

"If you mess around with his stuff, he will find out," their dad said. "He is an excellent detective. Can't hide anything from that man. I could never get away with anything when I was a kid. He'd always catch me if I messed with his stuff."

"We aren't trying to hide anything," said Alice, exasperated.

"I didn't think you were. I was talking to your brother." Her dad gave her a long stare. "Are you sure you're not hiding anything?" he said. He stared at her hard. Then a smile formed on his lips and, not able to hold it in, he laughed.

"Really funny, dad," said Alice. "Mom, can we *please* go to our room?"

Their mom sighed, "Ok."

The Forbidden Treasure

Alice and Jax jumped up from the table, but before they could rush off, their mom grabbed them and hugged them.

"I know you don't like Mystery Lake," their mom said. "But this is our home. You need to accept that."

"Ok, I'll try." Alice lied through her teeth.

* * * *

On the third day at their new school, they managed to make it to lunch without being called into the principal's office. It looked like Jen might not have told on them.

But Alice was still anxious. *Maybe the principal was just waiting till the end of the day. He had to fill out their expulsion papers before he talked to them. Maybe Jen was going to try and blackmail them.*

Alice looked down at her lunch with distaste. *Peanut butter and jelly and some tortilla chips? You know what, I'm not really hungry anymore. And why would I want tortilla chips with peanut butter and jelly, dad?* she thought bitterly. She was fuming with anger, and Jen had come over just to make her feel worse.

Jen and her friends Katie and Mason sat down together. "Hey, Jax," Jen said. "How's it going?"

Jax looked up at her. "What do you want?"

I knew nobody would care about me. Stupid Jen, you just came over to this disgusting table to separate me and Jax. Alice just wanted to get out of this horrid cafeteria and outside where she would never have to breathe in air that smells like a garbage truck.

"I don't know why you're so mean," said Jen.

What? thought Alice. *Me, mean? Jen was obviously the mean one.*

"We used to be friends," said Jen. "You remember that."

"Yeah," said Jax. "You used to be cool."

"I haven't changed," Jen said. "I was so excited to hear that you were moving here. I missed you so much when I had to move. But then you get here and you act like you're too good for me."

"You're the one who's been acting stuck up," said Alice.

"Really," said Jen. "I tried to help you. I tried to be nice. You've just been mean."

Alice threw her chips into her lunch box and glared at Jen. "We don't want any help from you. And what happened to you?" she asked in a ferocious tone. "You've changed. You were a friend, but you've been nothing but rude to me since I got here. So what if we don't want to be your friend anymore? You've already made plenty of friends. And I'm not the one who's acting like they're too good for anybody else."

"*So what?!*" said Jen. "I am not a bad person, Alice. I want to help you. I try to be a good friend. I…"

The Forbidden Treasure

"YOU KNOW WHAT, JEN? I HAD TO LEAVE MY FRIENDS IN SAN FRANCISCO. AND I STILL HAVE TO GET USED TO STUPID MYSTERY LAKE!" Alice shouted with fire in her eyes.

The cafeteria was instantly quiet. Everyone turned to stare at Alice, who shrank down into her seat, embarrassed by the attention.

Jen didn't shout back. She just sat there with a small smile on her face.

The excitement was apparently over, and everyone turned back to their own lunch and conversations.

"Meet me at the old abandoned mansion across from your house after school," Jen said. "You can get in through the coal chute at the back of the house." She stood up and left.

Alice just wanted to slap her in the face . . . until that moment.

Alice paced up and down the block thinking about what to do. *What time was it?* she wondered. *Was that her mom's car? No. When did her mom get home? Had she been pacing up and down the block for 30 minutes?*

Jax had gone straight home, and their dad would probably be worrying about her. Alice didn't want her dad worrying. She needed to hurry home. And fast.

She sprinted down the block. Finally, she was home. She darted towards the door and turned the knob. "DAAAAD! I'm home!" she shouted.

Her dad looked up from the book he was reading. "Ok. Come on in. Get yourself a snack if you want. Don't mess up the house, I just finished cleaning—your Uncle Tony is coming over to say hi." He went back to his book.

"Uncle Tony's coming over?"

"Yeah—why aren't you with your brother? I thought you went with him to Jen's house." "What?"

"Glad you two are finally making friends…"

The door slammed behind Alice as she rushed back out of the house.

They wouldn't be at Jen's house, thought Alice. *They'd be at the old mansion.* Alice stood in the middle of the street, staring at the decrepit old building looming over her. *I can't believe Jax was talking to Jen when I told him not to. I can't believe he went without me.*

The Forbidden Treasure

Jax knew what he was doing. He wanted help, and he knew Alice was just being stubborn. And he knew that if he went first, she'd follow him; there was no way she was going to let him have all the fun.

Alice searched the backside of the house for the coal chute. She wasn't even sure what a coal chute was, but figured she'd know it when she saw it. There at the base of the wall was a board that looked like it was covering a window; it was loose. Alice swung the board away from the wall and there was a metal door. It creaked open with little effort. She looked into the inky shadows of the basement, dimly lit by what little sunshine managed to find its way in.

Why didn't I bring a flashlight?

Alice gingerly lowered her feet through the door. There was some sort of metal slide there. She took a breath and let herself go. Whoosh, thump. She was in the basement, sitting on the concrete floor.

Alice picked herself up, searched with her hands in the darkness, trying to get her bearings and not bump her head.

Her eyes began to adjust and she could see what looked like a door. There appeared to be a faint light on the other side of it. She made her way to the door, being careful not to smash her shins on some hidden trap.

She reached the door and pushed it open.

There in the middle of the floor sitting on a rug was Jen, Katie, and Mason—AND JAX.

The room was lit by a few small candles. On the wall was a big handmade sign that read: *The Detective Club*.

"Oh, hey, Alice," said Jax. "I knew you'd make it. I was just telling them about the time machine, and showing them some sketches I drew."

The Forbidden Treasure

Willard

~ Chapter 5 ~

A Mystery Revealed

The Detective Club, Alice, and Jax (they had not been formally inducted into the club) walked through the library towards an enormous display case.

Jen led the way. "I've got something to show you," she said. "You won't believe it."

"More unbelievable than a time machine?" Jax scoffed.

"Maybe," Jen replied. She pointed to the center of the display case. "Look."

Alice's eyes widened. It was her shoe!

Or it had been. Now it was a fossil. But it very clearly appeared to be a shoe, the very one that Alice had just lost in the mud yesterday—well, I guess it was actually about 60 million years ago.

"But how?" asked Alice.

"Nobody ever had a good explanation," Jen replied. "Of course, they say it just looks like a shoe, but couldn't possibly really be a fossilized shoe. A gold miner found it about a hundred years ago. That's why this place is called Mystery Lake."

"Alice, that's yours," said Jax.

"How could that be her shoe?" asked Mason.

"With a time machine, of course," said Jen. "I knew it had to be something strange to cause that loud bang I heard, and the flash of light. And you two came stumbling out of that thing all muddy, and I thought—why's Alice wearing only one shoe? That's awfully weird."

"You believe them?" Katie asked.

"We'll see for sure when they get us in that room and show us how it works," said Jen.

"I'm not going back where any dinosaurs are!" Jax exclaimed.

"Follow me," said Jen. She led them over to another area of the display case.

"Hey, that's the mansion," said Alice.

The Forbidden Treasure

There was a huge black and white picture of the old abandoned mansion that sat across the street from them. But in the picture it was brand new. It stood on top of a knoll with a large open field surrounding it and an orchard behind it. A caption below the picture read "McQueen Manor, 1865." On the front steps stood a tall man—it must have been the owner.

"This is where I want to go," said Jen.

"Why? We were just in the basement," said Jax.

"That is Alistair McQueen," Jen said. She pointed at a portrait of the same tall man, which hung beside the picture of the mansion.

Alice looked at the portrait. Alistair McQueen was a stern-looking man. It was so hard to tell with these old pictures what someone was like. They had to stand as still as possible for so long or else they'd look all blurry. It was impossible to capture a smile, so everyone looked mean, or a bit stupid.

There's something strange about his eyes, thought Alice. *I'll bet he had some good stories to tell.*

"McQueen," said Jen, "was a world-famous explorer and treasure hunter. He travelled all over the world, discovered a tribe in the jungles of South America, fought in numerous wars— usually just to get his hands on some treasure. He came here for gold. Here he finally got filthy rich, finding a huge hoard of gold; he ran a large mine, built that big house. And then, one day, he and all his gold just disappeared."

"We've been researching him for over a year," said Katie.

"That's what our Detective Club's been doing," said Mason.

"We've been trying to find clues that would help us figure out what happened to him," Katie continued.

"You want to find Alistair McQueen?" asked Alice.

"We want to find his gold," Jen replied.

"That's crazy," said Jax. "You just said he fought in wars just to try and get rich. You think you're going to be able to take his gold?"

"Yeah, that would be crazy," said Jen. "We're not trying to take his gold from him. We want to find out where he left it, then we can get it."

"You don't think someone else found it," said Alice, "and that's why it disappeared?"

"That's where a time machine would come in handy," said Jen. "We can see what happened to it. Then even if someone else found it, we can always use the time machine to go back before they can take it."

"Let's go see if this time machine really works," said Mason.

* * * *

The Forbidden Treasure

Getting all five of them at once into the machine was a bit of a squeeze. And then it took a bit of working out to figure out what number they should set it to. But after some figuring, they settled on - .000165.

They pressed the big button in the middle of the control panel, and then BANG!

"I can't believe it worked," said Mason.

"I told you it did," said Jax. "I'm not a liar."

"Don't you think we should get ourselves some different clothing?" said Alice.

"Probably should have thought of that before we jumped back in time to here," said Jax.

"I wanted to see how it worked before I invested my allowance into a bunch of old timey costumes," replied Jen. "Besides, nobody seems to care."

Which was true. Five young children walking down the muddy road of a mining camp was unusual. But none of the miners seemed to care. This was a boomtown: hundreds of tents spread haphazardly in all directions. The muddy road led to a main street, which was evidently *the* main street, because it actually had some wooden buildings: a general store, a saloon, a post and telegraph office, and a bank. Along with the miners, a few pioneer families were settling in.

They saw a few children playing in a nearby field. A couple of families were gathered around a stump, discussing something of great importance, no doubt. A wagon full of lumberjacks trundled by, heading towards the woods. A miner was passed out in the middle of the road.

Jax was so engrossed by the scene he walked straight into the back of a man who had just come out of the general store, which sent the man's tools clattering to the ground.

"Oh, sorry," said Jax.

The man picked up the shovel and pickaxe he had dropped. "No bother, son," he said.

The children all stared at the man. There was something very familiar about him.

The Forbidden Treasure

The man looked them over for a moment. "Better be getting back to your father," he said. Then he turned and went on his way.

"That was Alistair McQueen," Jen whispered. "Come on, let's follow him." Not waiting for the others, she started after McQueen.

It was not long till they came to a large crowd, and McQueen disappeared amongst all the people.

"Did you see where he went?" said Jen. "I can't believe we lost him. When she turned back to the groups, she was surprised to see the looks of terror on their faces. She turned to see what they were all looking at.

In the middle of the crowd stood a gallows. On the gallows five Native Americans were about to be hung. On the steps leading up to the gallows, at least another five waited, shackled to each other.

The hangman finished putting a noose and hood on the last man. A soldier began to read out a statement.

"These savages have been a menace to our community. They have been convicted of 18 counts of murder. For their crimes they will be hung by the neck until dead…"

A cheer went up from the crowd.

"Kill the murderers!" a miner shouted.

"We need to get out of here now!" said Alice. She grabbed Jax's hand.

"This is horrible," said Katie.

"Come on," said Alice.

They turned away from the gallows and shoved through the crowd that pressed in around them.

"You don't want to miss this," said a pioneer woman, as they pushed past her.

The kids escaped the crowd and began to run back the way they came.

"What is wrong with those people?" said Kate. "Why would they want to watch that?"

"Were they really murderers?" asked Mason.

"Let's just get home," said Alice. "I don't want to be here anymore."

The Forbidden Treasure

Willard

~ Chapter 6 ~

Alistair McQueen

The children ran back the way they came, down the muddy road. The way was now nearly deserted and the tent city empty; everyone must have gone to witness the hanging.

After about a half mile, Jen slowed up to a walk. "Stop," she said, gasping for air. "We…" she struggled to catch her breath, "…don't need to run all the way."

The others stopped running.

Katie was the last to stop, reluctantly. If she hadn't been more afraid to be alone, she would have kept on running. "I want to get home now!"

"Just slow down. I'm not a track star like you," said Jen.

"Just please hurry," said Katie.

"What did you expect it to be like?" asked Jen.

"I don't remember reading anything about hangings around here," said Mason, as he shivered.

"Of course there'd be hangings," said Jen. "That's what they did. Haven't you ever seen a western movie?"

"That's different," said Katie. "Those aren't real."

"Yeah, it's worse," said Jax.

They trudged on through the mud, nearing the edge of the tent city. They could see the woods where they knew the time machine would be waiting for them.

"I don't want to go back yet," said Jen.

"I'm not going to stay here. This place is going to give me nightmares," Katie said.

Jen stopped. "You can wait by the time machine, but I still want to find Alistair."

"We need to stick together," said Alice.

"Yeah," said Jax, "splitting up is not a good idea."

"Someone could get stuck here," added Alice.

"I don't think this is the right time," said Mason. "We went too far back. He must have just shown up here—that's why he was buying supplies. He wouldn't have found any gold yet."

"You may be right," Jen admitted. "But we need to figure out what he's up to."

A miner stepped out of a nearby tent. "Who are you looking for?" he asked. "Maybe I can help."

The children all turned to look at the man. It was Alistair. "Hey," he said, "you're the kids who ran into me in town."

"We're looking for our father," Alice blurted out.

Alistair looked the kids over. "You are all brothers and sisters?"

"Uh, yes," said Alice.

"You sure don't look like it."

"Well, we are," said Alice.

"Did I hear you say your father's name is Alistair?"

"Yes, sir," said Jen.

"Quite a coincidence. My name is Alistair."

"Really," said Jen. "That is funny."

"Where are you children from? You don't look like any pioneer children I've ever seen before. I've been all over the world and I don't think I've ever seen folks dressed quite like you—though I have seen girls wearing pants, just not around here."

"We're from Finland," said Jax.

"Finland!?" said Alice. "Uh, yeah, Finland."

"Interesting," Alistair said. "I have never been there. You speak very good English, though I've never heard an accent like yours either. Is that a Finnish accent?"

"Well," Jax responded, "I say we are from Finland, but our father is English, so we don't actually speak Finnish."

"Good save," Mason whispered.

"I think our father is watching the hanging," said Jen. "We lost him in the crowd. Can we wait here?"

Alistair considered the request. "Would you like some coffee?"

"Yes, please, sir," said Jen.

"Pull up a log by the fire there." Alistair pointed at a nearby pit, where a fire smoldered in a pile of coals. "I'll get some coffee. Can you get that fire stoked, boy?" Alistair said to Jax.

"Uh, yes, sir."

Jax got the fire going, and Alistair quickly returned from inside his tent with a metal pot and mugs. He set the pot by the fire to percolate, and sat down on a log.

Alistair looked around the fire. All of the children, except Jen, were looking into the fire; Jen gazed expectantly back at him. "What is your name?"

"Jen. I mean, Jennifer."

"I should warn you, Jennifer, the coffee is not very good. I hope that won't be a disappointment."

"Oh, no, sir, that's fine. Please, if you don't mind, are you Alistair McQueen?"

"Yes, I am."

"Alistair McQueen, the great adventurer, who's traveled the world searching for treasure?"

"How would you know that?"

Alice kicked Jen's foot.

Jen kicked back and gave Alice a glare. She quickly looked back to Alistair with a smile on her face. "I read about you in a dime novel."

"Really? I didn't think anyone had yet considered any of my discoveries worth telling the world about."

"Oh, yes. It was a very interesting story about a golden statue you discovered in Africa."

"That!" Alistair carefully picked up the coffee pot so as not to burn himself and poured each of them a cup of coffee. "I see. That was a pretty good find. Sold it to the British Museum."

"It said you had to fight a pack of ferocious baboons barehanded."

"Well, no," said Alistair. "That's dime novels for you."

Alice took a sip of coffee and instantly spat it out with a cough and splutter.

"I told you it wasn't very good. Let me get some sugar." Alistair got up and went into his tent.

Alice turned to Jen. "What are you doing?" she demanded.

"What we came here for," Jen hissed back, "research."

"He already thinks we're weird," said Alice. "You're going to give us away."

"You think he's going to figure out we're from the future and came here in a time machine?" said Jen.

"Jen's right," said Jax. "He won't figure anything out. He couldn't even comprehend it. We get him talking about himself, and he probably won't even think about who we are."

"Shut up!" Mason whispered, as Alistair emerged from the tent.

"Here's that sugar," Alistair said, and dumped a couple spoonfuls into everyone's cups. "There, that will be better." He sat back on his log, and pulled something glinty from his coat pocket. "Would you like to see the greatest treasure I ever found? Discovered it on a trip deep into the Caucasus Mountains."

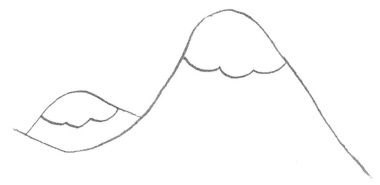

"Please," said Jen.

"Where's that?" asked Jax.

"The Caucasus?" said Alistair. "Are a mountain range on the far eastern edge of Europe, forming a wall against Asia.

It's there I found this amulet." Holding fast to the chain, Alistair let an enormous emerald set in gold fall from his hand and dangle in front of the children's faces.

"Can I hold it?" Jen begged.

"Better not," Alistair replied. "It's not safe."

Jen looked very disappointed.

"You see, it's cursed."

"You wouldn't believe in some silly superstition like that, would you?" Jen asked.

Alistair took a long drink of his coffee. "It's no superstition. I lost my traveling companion to this thing."

"What happened?" asked Alice.

"First, I need to tell you how I found it," said Alistair. "My partner Charles and I had traveled through Europe for months—from England to France, slowly making our way through the continent, with some very fruitful stops in Prague, Romania, the Ukraine." He took another drink of his coffee. "But those are stories for another day.

"We were traveling on the Silk Road through the Caucasus, hoping to make it eventually to Beijing. But our progress had been slow; the distractions had been many. I have always found it difficult to pass up an opportunity for adventure. As a result, we found ourselves still in the mountains as winter was setting in. I can still remember the day, November 2, 1827. A blizzard caught our caravan in a dangerous pass. Our wagons were stuck. We unhitched our horses and searched for nearby shelter. Fortunately, we stumbled across a monastery.

"It was just in time. The snow was piling up, darkness was closing in around us. In the thick forest we had lost our way. Charles was slumped over on his horse, nearly dead from exposure. And then I saw a glimmer of light, faint, but certainly a flicker. I trudged through the snow leading the horses along, practically dragging them, forcing them not to give up.

"The monastery was small, housing only a few monks. They served a rather insignificant and rarely-used chapel. But the monks were very gracious. They did not have much to share, but they shared everything they had. And after nursing Charles back to health, they let us remain with them over the winter, until it became safe to continue our journey.

"I spent most of my time cutting wood for the fires, and reading in the library. What a magnificent library it was. Not that it was opulent—that is to say, fancy—but they had a splendid selection of such a wide variety of books. In one of those books covering local folklore, I found a story about this very amulet. And it was at that very monastery, in their chapel, that the amulet was kept. The emerald had come from the mountains of Afghanistan. Some said it was cursed, others that it brought fortune to those who possessed it."

The Forbidden Treasure

"You stole it from a church!" exclaimed Alice.

"Now, don't interrupt," Alistair replied. "I'll get to that." He continued, "I asked the abbot if I could see it. He wondered how I knew of the amulet, and I told him about how I had read about it in the library. To which he replied that they were not familiar with that book. It was a very old monastery, and the books had been collected over hundreds of years. He told me the amulet had been in the chapel for as long as anyone knew. They had forgotten how it had come to be there. They just knew it had belonged to Saint Helena—she was the mother of the Roman Emperor Constantine the Great.

"It was kept in a reliquary in the chapel. It was a rather small and modest chapel, but covered in beautiful, vibrant paintings—and there at the side of the chapel was a small statue and icon of St. Helena. And beside it, suspended by its chain, hanging in a glass box, was this amulet.

"It called out to me. I mean that literally: I heard a voice say to me, 'Alistair McQueen, free me from this prison. Free me and I will bless you with prosperity beyond your wildest dreams.' I turned to the abbot, and it was clear that he had heard no voice.

"I thought I was losing my mind. But every time I visited the chapel, I heard the voice again. It called to me, promised me riches, begged to be free. I couldn't take it. If I wasn't crazy, I thought this would drive me crazy. So even though I felt drawn to it, I refused to go into the chapel.

"The winter months passed, the snow was melting, any day it would be safe to leave. Charles was ready, but I kept putting it off another day. I couldn't bring myself to leave the amulet."

He locked eyes with Alice. "But I couldn't steal it."

"Then one night, as I was fast asleep, I saw her: the most glorious woman I have ever seen. I asked her name, but she couldn't tell me. But I recognized her voice. It was the voice from the amulet. 'St. Helena?' I asked. She shook her head no. 'What do you want?' I asked.

'Freedom', she said. Then smoke and flames rose from beneath her; they engulfed her.

"Suddenly, I was being shaken awake by Charles. The monastery was on fire. We rushed from the building. To my horror I saw that the chapel was on fire as well. The monks had given up fighting the blaze. They stood and watched helplessly. But I couldn't just watch. I rushed into the chapel, I found the amulet, and I saved it.

"For my bravery, the abbot allowed me to keep it. He said it was mine to protect and steward.

"We left the monastery three weeks later, joining a passing caravan. But only four days into our journey, I woke to find Charles had disappeared. He had taken a horse and supplies and had run away. Then I discovered the amulet was missing; he had stolen it.

"I tracked him for months. When I finally caught up to him in China, it was only to find his grave. He had found refuge in a Buddhist temple. The monks there had been kind enough to care for him in his last days. They told me he had gone mad, and he would spend all day jabbering on about this amulet. It spoke to him, he told them. It was all the amulet's fault, he said. It was the amulet that had made him do so many terrible things.

"The monks happily returned the amulet to me when I told them I was the rightful owner. I am the chosen steward, and so I must protect it. I never wear it, but I always keep it in my pocket, so that no one like Charles will ever steal it again."

"What's the point of that?" said Jen. "Not much of a treasure if you can't do anything with it."

"That is where you are wrong," Alistair replied. "That's the best kind of treasure. I've had to be extra careful lately; my new assistant, Anthony, has been a little too nosy about it—but he is good at finding gold."

"Your assistant's name is Anthony?" asked Alice.

"Yes," said Alistair. "Have you met him?" "Where is he?" said Alice.

"I'm not sure. I think he went to town."

"Well, thank you for the coffee, and the story," said Jax. "But I think it's time for us to get going. Ok, Jen?"

"O k?" said Alistair. "Your accent is so interesting. What is o k?"

"Alright," said Jen. "It means alright." She turned to Alice. "I think we learned what we needed."

"What's that?" Alistair asked.

"Oh," Jen replied, "we just wanted to find out who lived in these tents. Our family just moved to the area, and just wanted to know who else lived here."

Jax put down his mug and stood up. Alice and the others followed his lead.

"I see," said Alistair. "Well, stop by anytime."

"Thank you," said Alice.

The Forbidden Treasure

Willard

~ Chapter 7 ~

Back Again

"So do we get to be in your Detective Club?" asked Jax.

Jax and Alice sat in the basement of the old mansion, in a circle with Jen, Mason, and Katie. It was late. Only a candle lit the room.

"Yeah," said Jen. "You can be in our club."

"But you're in charge, right?" said Alice. "We've got to do whatever you say?"

"No," Jen shot back. "I'm not some jerk, Alice. I'm not going to make anyone do anything they don't want to do."

"Well, I'm not going back in that time machine!" said Katie. She stood up and started pacing. "I hate it."

"Yeah, that place was horrible," said Mason.

"It was amazing!" said Jen. "That was the coolest thing that's ever happened to us. Now we can solve some real mysteries."

"Those people got killed," said Katie.

Jen slumped. "I'm not saying that was great, obviously," she said, looking at the ground, ashamed. "That was terrible. But what can we do about that?"

"I'm not going back there," said Mason. "Maybe some other year, but not then."

"Sounds like Jax and I are your Detective Club now," said Alice.

"I'll still help," said Katie. "But I'm not doing any more time travel."

Jax looked around at each of them. They all looked at least a little scared, even Alice, who he could tell was trying to act braver than she was. "What's next then?"

There was a long pause.

Jen spoke first. "We don't go back so far. We need to go back to after Alistair built this house; we need to figure out exactly when his gold disappeared and go back to then."

"We need to figure out exactly how the numbers work on the machine," said Alice.

"I'll help with that," said Mason. "I'm good at math."

"What about Uncle Tony?" said Jax.

"What about him?" asked Jen.

"Alistair's assistant, Anthony," said Jax. "Uncle Tony is the one with a time machine. He must be using it too. It must be him."

"Well, if it is, there might be pictures of him," said Jen. "We'll look through all the old books from that time and see if it is him."

Katie stopped pacing, "I can help with that."

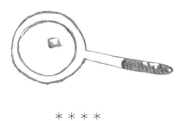

* * * *

Over the next few weeks, the junior detectives spent every extra moment they had in the library, and local museum. They discovered that Alistair had been a prominent member of the community, being a generous patron—meaning he gave away a lot of money—to many local organizations up until 1889. In November of 1889, he left town one night with nothing more than a horse, a pair of saddle bags, and the clothes he was wearing.

But there was no money, no gold, no jewels (or amulets) left behind. He did leave behind a handful of very large unpaid debts. McQueen Manor and its furnishings were sold, but this only covered part of the debt. So Alice argued he must have lost all his money well before November, but it was hard to determine exactly when this had happened.

After looking through numerous old books, and even having to inspect a roll of microfiche—which was an ordeal, because they first had to figure out what microfiche was, and then convince the librarian to pull the old microfiche machine out of the basement for them to use—they still had not found a photo that gave them any idea who Alistair's assistant Anthony was, and certainly couldn't prove he was in fact their Uncle Tony.

So they decided to use a different old detective's tool: they'd just follow Uncle Tony around until they saw him use the time machine. Of course, this was easier to say than it was to do. Because, as you've probably experienced, it is very difficult for young children to convince their parents to let them wander around town at night. And it's hard to perform a stakeout without getting permission from your parents to be out late at night.

Alice and Jax looked for every excuse to spend time with their uncle, including inviting themselves over to his house for sleepovers. Finally, with a little help from their mom and dad—who were eager to have a night out without them—Uncle Tony relented and let the twins stay over.

"Alright," said Uncle Tony, "You've watched *Flight of the Navigator* three times through. I know it's a classic, but it's time for you to go to bed."

The Forbidden Treasure

"One more time, please," begged Alice.

"No, your parents are not going to be pleased with me if I let you stay up any later. You need to get some sleep for your soccer game tomorrow." Uncle Tony pulled Alice up from the couch. "Jax, I know you're playing opossum." Uncle Tony pulled the blanket off of Jax, who was sprawled out on the floor. "Come on, get up."

"Noooo," Alice whined, as Uncle Tony pushed her and Jax up the stairs to their bedroom.

"You stayed up long enough; besides, I have some work I still need to get done before I go to bed. So, you've kept me up too late as well."

"We like to watch you work," said Jax. "We could have helped you."

"Not with this. It's just papers that need to be graded. I can't save them all for Sunday night."

Maybe it was just papers to grade. But maybe it was time traveling he was going to get up to. The twins gave no more resistance. This was exactly what they wanted. They had already planned to just pretend to be asleep and then spy on their uncle.

The movie and treats had distracted them, but now they were back on course.

"There you go." Uncle Tony tucked them into bed. "Do you need any water?"

"No, thank you," said Alice.

Uncle Tony kissed them each on the forehead. "Do you need anything?

"Don't worry about us," said Jax. "We won't bother you."

For a moment it seemed like Uncle Tony was going to leave the door open a crack, but then he changed his mind, and pulled it shut.

The children waited silently, both straining to hear what their uncle might be up to, wondering how long they should wait till they got up.

They waited for what seemed like an hour. (It had been 15 minutes.)

"Do you hear anything?" whispered Jax.

"Nothing," Alice whispered back. "Do you think it's safe to get up?"

"Let's do it. If he sees us, we'll just tell him we're looking for the bathroom."

"Together? And we know where the bathroom is. That's not a good excuse."

"Then what do we say?"

"We'll just tell him we need some water."

The twins tiptoed through the darkened house. A light was on in their uncle's office. But when they cautiously approached, they couldn't hear him.

Jax peeked into the office. "He's not there."

Alice entered the office. "You stay and watch out for Uncle Tony," said Alice. Maybe there was something in here that would give them a clue. Alice scanned the office.

She gasped. His desk drawer, the one that was always locked, was ajar. Alice rushed over to the desk. She opened the drawer.

She gasped again. Her eyes grew wide. Her mouth hung open. Was that the amulet Alistair McQueen had kept in his pocket?! Had their uncle stolen it from Alistair?! Her face burned with anger. She glared. She couldn't believe that her uncle was a thief like Charles, but maybe he was a big liar.

"Jax, Uncle Tony stole the amulet." Her voice shook with rage.

"Alice."

"What?" Alice said to Jax, "Why are you talking so weird?"

"I didn't say anything," said Jax.

"Alice," something whispered softly, in a harsh crackly voice.

"You didn't say that?" asked Alice.

"Say what?" said Jax.

"You called my name."

"What are you talking about?" Jax was exasperated. He was hurriedly searching through the office. He didn't have time for stupid jokes.

"Aliiicccee."

"Did you hear that?" asked Alice.

"Hear what?" said Jax. Now he was getting worried.

"It is I, the creature of the mountain."

What? A horrifying realization washed over Alice. She slowly turned from Jax, turning back to the drawer and the amulet.

"Yes! You understa…"

Alice slammed the drawer shut. "Come on, Jax, let's get out of here."

Just then they heard Uncle Tony fling open the back door and stumble into the house. Something crashed to the ground. Uncle Tony cursed and grumbled, and began to pick whatever he dropped up.

"We need to hide," said Jax.

"We can't hide in here!" exclaimed Alice.

"He'll see us if we go into the hall."

"No," said Alice, desperate.

"Don't worry," said the thing in the drawer—whatever it was. "I won't tell on you, I won't tell him you're hiding, you can trust me."

Alice did not trust the thing, but Jax was right; Uncle Tony would see them if they went into the hall. They could try to go out the window, but then they might get locked outside. And they didn't have time, Uncle Tony was coming…

"Come on," said Jax. He had found a spot behind a couch and armchair in the corner of the room where they could tuck themselves in. He pulled Alice down next to him. "Be absolutely silent."

The Forbidden Treasure

Jax really didn't need to tell Alice that. She knew. And she would be, because she was terrified.

Uncle Tony shoved open the office door.

Alice could just see him through a sliver between the arm of the couch and the arm of the chair.

He looked strangely different. Not the quiet and nice Uncle Tony. Sure, most people wouldn't have thought of him as the friendliest man. But he was very kind to his niece and nephew, and anyone who took the time to know him. But now he looked crazed: he was covered in dirt, his hair was a mess, anger flashed in his eyes. And he was carrying five huge—I mean really big—gold nuggets.

"Good," said the thing in the drawer. "You found it."

"Yes, I did everything you told me to do," said Uncle Tony. He struggled to carry the nuggets across the room without dropping them again, and he put them down in front of a large safe next to his desk. He spun the dial on the safe, working out the combination.

"That is not all the gold."

"It was all I could carry!" Uncle Tony opened the safe and began placing the nuggets inside. "That's the final stash, buried deeper than I thought it'd be…"

"We had to make sure no one else found our treasure."

"*My* treasure!"

"Yes, yes, your treasure. I am merely your slave."

"Don't forget it!" shouted Uncle Tony. He slammed the safe shut. "You're always trying to tell me what to do. I'm in charge. I decide what I do."

"I would never want to tell you what to do. I am here to serve you. You wanted to steal the gold, you wanted to cheat Alistair, it was you. You want to destroy this town."

"What! When did I say that?! I'm a scientist. I *need* the gold. I'm going to save the world. We must find a way to get to Mars. We must be able to colonize it. It's the only way to save the earth. I want to save people. Alistair just wanted to build big houses, and railroads, and make himself richer. He didn't care about anyone but himself. I'm going to save the world!"

"Yes, yes, I believe in you. But we mustn't let anyone stop you. They don't understand how smart you are. They don't understand what you can accomplish. They will think you are bad, and they will try to take away everything you've done, and everything you will do to save them. They are stupid, and cannot be trusted."

Uncle Tony dropped onto the coach, exhausted. "I can't trust anyone; I can't let anyone stop me."

"Yes, yes," said the thing—the creature from the depths of the mountain. "No one can stop us."

"No one can stop us," repeated Uncle Tony.

"Now go get all of my gold," demanded the creature.

Uncle Tony picked himself up off the couch. "Yes," he replied. "We must have it all," he said as he plodded out of the room.

The twins sat absolutely still, waiting and listening, till they heard the back door shut behind him.

"He's gone," Alice heard the creature's voice say in her head.

"Let's get out of here now!" she cried and bolted from behind the couch.

Jax rushed after her.

"There's no need to run," said the creature.

But Alice didn't stop running till they were back in their room. She leapt into her bed and pulled the covers up over her head.

"Who was Uncle Tony talking to?" asked Jax. "That was really weird."

"You didn't hear that voice!" said Alice. "It was like it was crawling into my brain."

"Uncle Tony's voice?" asked Jax.

"No! It called itself the creature from the depths of the mountains."

"What? I didn't hear that."

"I think it was the amulet. Just like Alistair said. It's cursed. There's something in it. It's making Uncle Tony crazy and getting him to do bad things."

"Bad things? Was that Alistair's gold?"

"This is way worse than we thought. We have to stop Uncle Tony or he's going to destroy the town. We have to go back. We have to stop whatever that evil spirit is trying to make him do."

The Forbidden Treasure

A gift for you

Happy Birthday, Jojo! Aunt Ginny and Uncle mark From Aunt Ginny

~ Chapter 8 ~

Nunquam Non Paratus[1]

Alice headed in the direction of the cafeteria. Her lunch box banged against her knees as she walked alone, trying to avoid anyone who crossed her path. She thought about the voice, the amulet, the gold, and Uncle Tony, and became angry. She never thought he could be a thief. That story Alistair told. Charles seemed like such a coward. How could Uncle Tony be like that?

Now she had heard that voice in her head. What did that mean about her? She trudged down the hall, while her boots squeaked on the tile floor.

When she reached the cafeteria, she took a seat next to Katie. She unpacked her lunch. *Yuck*.

---

[1] Never Not Prepared

She watched Jax and the others talking over each other about the gold.

Why did we have to move here? she thought. *This place is packed with mysteries, but why so many? And half of them could destroy this town.*

"Maybe he turned into, uh, you know, a Mr. Hyde," said Jax. "Like Dr. Jekyl and Mr. Hyde. You know, Alice, like the old cartoons our dad showed us. He drinks some sort of potion and it turns him into a monster. It could be possible. He looked like a caveman. I mean why else would he look so crazy?"

"Duh," said Katie. "Because he's nuts. That's why a person looks crazy, cause they are."

"He's not nuts," protested Jax.

"Yeah huh," Katie continued.

"No, he isn't!" Alice snapped.

Katie glared at Alice, and scooted just a little bit away from her.

"Well, I found something interesting in the museum. I was there all-day Saturday," said Mason. "There was this big train robbery, just outside of town. It happened only a few months before Alistair left. Nobody ever got caught. Someone blew up the locomotive and derailed the train. Nobody even knows why, because there wasn't supposed to be anything valuable on it. So it was really strange that some gang would attack it like that."

Mason paused to make sure everyone was paying close attention. He was really proud of what he found.

"What I think," he said, "I think Alistair was trying to sneak his gold out of town. Your uncle would have known about it. And he stole the gold from the train."

"That's just some wild guess," said Jax.

Mason's pride deflated.

"It could be true," said Katie. "Makes as much sense as you."

"It's just an idea," said Mason.

"How about you all just shut up." Jen declared fiercely. "Anyways, that doesn't even make sense."

"I don't know how he did it," interrupted Alice, "but Uncle Tony stole the gold, he stole the amulet, and he hid it all so he could get it now."

"We saw it," said Jax.

"How are we going to stop him?" asked Jen. "We don't know when he went back."

"Then we start before when we think Alistair must have lost his money, and we work our way back," said Jax. "We have a time machine. We can take all the time it takes."

"What are we going to do," said Jen, "when will we find him?"

"We have to get the amulet," said Alice. "We get that, we stop whatever is making him do all this stuff."

"Then we wouldn't need to worry about knowing when Uncle Tony stole the gold," said Jen. "We can take the amulet from Alistair."

"He'll probably remember you," said Mason.

"So then we have to steal the amulet from him," said Alice. "That won't be easy."

"I'll bet that if you go back after he's built his mansion," said Katie, "he won't be carrying that thing around in his pocket anymore. He'll probably have it in a safe in his house."

"How are we going to get it, then?" asked Jax.

"We'll be prepared this time," said Jen.

And so they would be.

* * * *

Jen, Jax, and Alice crowded into the time machine. It had taken them a week to gather up all the tools they figured they'd need.

Not knowing exactly what they'd face, they had researched how to break into a circa 1865 safe. There were plenty of videos on YouTube, since the only people these days who would likely be wanting to break into a safe that old are probably just antique hunters who have a legitimate reason trying to get into some old safe that no one had the combination to anymore, not someone trying to steal something valuable from a bank.

It didn't look very hard, really. Safes in the 1800s weren't really designed to be fortified against battery-powered drills with diamond-tipped bits, and sawzalls that can cut through metal with ease. Alice had borrowed the tools from her dad.

Then they had to get some clothes that were more appropriate to the times, so they wouldn't look so out of place. These they borrowed from the local children's museum.

And finally, they had borrowed Uncle Tony's keys to the school.

It was after 9:00 at night. The school was empty. They had no problem getting to the time machine. They were prepared, as best as they knew how to be. They were determined. They weren't coming back to this time until they had accomplished their mission. They would steal the amulet, and destroy it if they could. If they couldn't destroy it, they'd put it somewhere no one would ever find it.

* * * *

You, or the parent who might be reading this book to you, may at this point be wondering about the possibility of alternate realities being created if they manage to accomplish their mission. They were not wondering about this, because even though they had seen *Avengers: Endgame*, they had no idea what the movie meant when it tried to explain time travel.

So, we are not going to try to explain time travel either. We can simply say here that we don't believe in alternate timelines, or a multiverse. Most importantly, like our determined protagonists, we are sure that you can change the future, at least we hope so.

* * * *

The three kids silently crept into the school auditorium. There was only a faint noise of the cool night breeze blowing through the windows. Luckily, the cameras—which they hadn't thought about—were deactivated (budget cuts). They crept down the hallway, as quiet as the night.

With a *creeeaaak!* they opened the door to the science lab. They could hardly see the egg-shaped machine in the dimly-lit room.

Alice's head hurt looking at all those creepy dead animals, looking out with their creepy glass eyes. That told her this was wrong. But she didn't listen to those voices inside her head. She focused on her feet, taking small steps, not wanting to kick anything over as they inched through the nearly completely dark room.

Finally, standing right before them was the giant metal machine. When they were in, they carefully set the time to 1898, just after the mansion was built.

Alice carried the tools in an old burlap sack. They didn't want anyone to see them and get suspicious: it would probably mess up time if anybody saw their power tools in the 1800s.

Jax pushed the button. There was the flash of light and low rumble you could feel in your body even after you found yourself in a new location in time that they had grown used to. They all gasped for air the moment they arrived—it was like time travel sucked all the air out of your lungs. They gulped in air, and waited for the humming in their bodies to stop. When they finally felt they had their bodies back to normal, they stepped out of the machine.

As they walked down the dark muddy roads, the few people they passed paid no attention to them. They looked like three normal children, fitting right into the time. Three normal children out for a walk late at night. That may have aroused some suspicion, but not enough for anyone to care.

After getting their bearings in the slightly unusual landscape, they found McQueen Manor. To their surprise, Jax and Alice's house was under construction across the street. They had no idea their home was so old.

"I can't believe we're doing this," said Jen.

"We have to," said Alice. "It's the only way to stop whatever that thing is that's controlling Uncle Tony."

"What are we supposed to do when we get it?" Jax asked.

"We'll figure that out when we get it," said Alice. "Come on, let's find the coal chute."

Getting in through a coal chute is much dirtier when it's actually being used for coal. The children were covered in black dust. But they found that as they snuck through the house it helped them be much harder to see in the dim light of the oil lamps. That helped them hide from the searching eyes of the butler, who could have sworn he heard something in the hallway.

Now, he did hear something, but he saw nothing when he inspected what the noise might have been. And so the children snuck into Alistair McQueen's library, where they found a large safe.

"Let's hope it's in there," said Jax.

Alice put her index finger to her mouth—which, combined with the glare she gave Jax, clearly communicated: *don't talk.*

Alice set the bag full of tools down, and cautiously, as quiet as she could, pulled each tool out and laid them in front of the safe. She then pulled out a stack of papers that contained the notes they had taken from YouTube videos they'd watched on how to crack such a safe.

But then it occurred to all of them at the same time. How were they going to break into the safe without making noise? The moment they pulled the trigger on the drill, the butler would certainly come see what all the noise was.

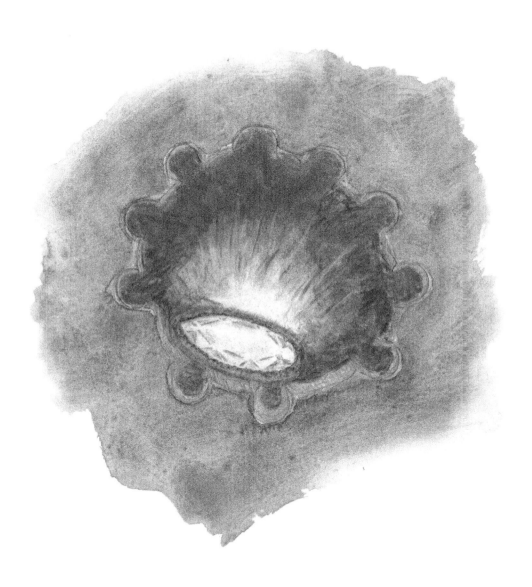

~ Chapter 9 ~

The Heist

"Can we talk?" whispered Jax.

"How are we going to do this?" whispered Jen.

"We're going to get caught as soon as we start."

Alice thought for a moment. They could lock the door, and put some other stuff in front of it to block it. That might keep people out long enough for them to break into the safe. But how would they get away? "We need to tie everyone up."

"Are you crazy?" exclaimed Jax. "How are we going to do that?"

"What other option do we have?" asked Alice.

They sat in silence, thinking.

"How many people are in the house?" asked Jen.

"I don't think we really have any idea," Alice responded.

"I don't think we planned this out nearly as well as we thought we did," said Jax.

Alice glared at him.

"What?" said Jax. "I'm just saying."

"Let's go look," said Alice.

The children crept slowly through the house, cautiously listening at each door. They'd listen for movement, for snoring, anything that sounded human. If they heard nothing, they'd slowly open the door and make sure.

After a thorough check of the house, they were convinced that the butler was the only person there. What was most certainly Alistair's bedroom was empty. It appeared that a cook did live at the home, but their bed was empty as well, as was the kitchen; so they too must be away somewhere else.

Now what would they do with the butler?

Alice stood at the front door. A kerosene torch gave enough light for her to see a bell hanging by the front door. She rang it. She waited. She rang it again.

A few moments later she could hear an angry butler making his way to the front door.

She waited.

The door swung open. "Who is calling at this hour? What do you want!" The butler held his lantern out towards Alice to get a good look at her.

The Forbidden Treasure

"I need help," said Alice.

"How dare… help? Help, how?"

"My father collapsed in the road. Please help him."

"Show me." The butler followed quickly after Alice as she hurried down the steps and out towards the road. He did not notice the little hop she took as she passed between two trees that lined the walk. And so he tripped over the rope that was stretched across the walkway.

Jax and Jen sprung from the nearby bushes and jumped on him.

"What is this!" the butler shouted, but fell silent when Jax knocked him over the head with a log.

"Jax!" exclaimed Alice.

"What? I had to shut him up." Jax stood over the butler, the log still in his hand, looking very worried about what he had just done.

"You could kill him, hitting him like that."

"I didn't hit him that hard, I swear."

"Shut up and help me tie him up," said Jen.

They set to tying up the butler's hands and feet, and used a bandana to gag him. Then with some effort they dragged him off the pathway and hid him in the bushes.

"Are we sure he won't just get up and run to get help as soon as he comes to?" asked Alice.

Jax untied the rope from between the two trees. He then tied the rope from the butler's feet and up to his hands behind his back. "There," said Jax. "He won't be going anywhere now."

"I feel sorry for him," said Jen.

"He'll be alright," said Jax, reassuring himself as much as the girls.

"Come on," said Alice. "Let's get back to that safe."

Now with no worry of making too much noise, they got to work with the drill. It was slow going, but they drilled one hole after another in the shape of a circle. Then by drilling every bit of metal out between two of the holes, they were able to get the sawzall into the circle and cut between each hole—making one big hole in the face of the safe large enough to reach a hand in.

Alice shone her flashlight through the hole into the safe. There it was—the glimmering green amulet. She reached into the safe and snatched the amulet. A strange feeling began to work its way up her arm, like a slime oozing across her skin, and fire tingling in her bones.

She quickly pulled the amulet from the safe and dropped it on the ground. "Don't touch it."

The children all stared at the amulet. Then Alice took a hammer and pushed the amulet, so she didn't have to touch it again, into the burlap sack. She shoved the other tools on top of it.

"Let's get out of here."

The children ran through the hall, down the steps, and straight towards the front door. But as they reached for the handle, it turned.

"This way," said Jax, and they all jumped into a side room, just in time to avoid Alistair who came through the front door helping the very confused and sore butler.

"You said it was a young girl?" said Alistair.

The butler rubbed his throbbing head. "But someone tripped me. And there must have been five other men who attacked me."

"Let's just get you to bed. I'm sure you need some rest," said Alistair, as he led the butler through to his room.

"That will be the last time I help someone," moaned the butler.

The children held their breath, motionless, until they heard the butler's bedroom door close. Then they sprung from their hiding place and ran out the front door.

They ran full speed down the muddy road back towards the time machine.

They had done it. They had the amulet. They hadn't been caught. They would figure out how to destroy it, or get rid of it, and then everything would be back to normal. And they probably should be done with this time-traveling business altogether.

They left the road and started into the woods. The time machine wasn't much further on.

"Oh!" yelled Jax as he fell to the ground.

"What's wrong?" asked Alice as she knelt down beside him. "Come on, get up."

"My ankle," said Jax. "I stepped in a hole."

"Can you walk?"

Jax pushed himself back to his feet. He took a step on his hurt ankle and fell again.

"No!"

"Let me help you." Alice helped Jax back to his feet. She pulled his arm over her shoulder. "I'll help you."

With Alice's help Jax began to limp slowly along the path. "Where's Jen?" asked Alice.

Jen had been in front of Jax and didn't hear him fall. She had kept running. Now she was wondering where Jax and Alice were. "Jax," she called out. "Alice."

"What are you doing here?!" said Uncle Tony.

Jen spun around, wide eyed, and there was Uncle Tony.

The Forbidden Treasure

Uncle Tony grabbed her by the shoulders. "How did you get here?"

"Wha, what do you mean?" said Jen. "I was just out for a walk."

Uncle Tony hesitated. Did she know where she was? "You're out for a walk?" "Yeah."

"Do you know what time it is?"

"Uh, 7:30."

"Why are you wearing a bonnet?"

"I was just playing dress up with some friends. We like to play *Little House on the Prairie*."

"What year is it?"

"What? What kind of question is that? We're just playing pioneers; I don't think I *am* one. It's 2011." *Oh yeah*, thought Jen. *Now I've got him, that'll confuse him, that was really smart.*

Uncle Tony took Jen by the hand. "Come on. You need to get home."

"Jen," Alice called out. She didn't want to shout, just in case someone else was out in the woods—or worse, in case Alistair was chasing them.

"She's got to just be up ahead of us," said Jax. "She'll probably be waiting for us at the time machine."

"I hope she didn't get lost," said Alice.

They trudged on through the woods, slowly, towards the time machine.

"Shouldn't we have been there by now?" asked Jax.

"I don't know," replied Alice. "It's so hard to see."

"Get out the flashlight."

"I don't know if that's a good idea."

"Don't worry, no one will see us."

Alice reached into the burlap bag and pulled out the flashlight, being careful not to touch the amulet. She turned it on and scanned the area. "I don't recognize anything."

"I remember that tree," said Jax. "It was right by the time machine when we came out. It should just be on the other side."

"Jen," Alice called out again. "Jen."

Alice and Jax hobbled along to the tree.

"It should be right over there," said Jax, pointing towards where the time machine had been.

Alice pointed the flashlight. But there was no time machine, just a large indent in the ground, which they both knew meant the time machine had been there and now was gone.

The Forbidden Treasure

Willard

~ Chapter 10 ~

Stuck in the Past

"You can open your eyes now," said Uncle Tony. "I'll walk you home."

Jen opened her eyes. They were outside of the school. "Why did I have to close my eyes?" she asked. Of course, she knew Uncle Tony had her close her eyes so she didn't see the time machine, but she thought it would be good to play dumb and act like she had no idea what might be going on.

So smart.

Uncle Tony hesitated. "Just some experiments I'm working on. Top secret things I'm working on for the government that no one can see. Sorry. Thank you for cooperating."

"I don't understand why we had to go through the school."

"Don't worry about it."

Jen figured that was enough acting dumb and didn't ask any more questions as they walked the rest of the way home.

They reached Jen's home. "Here you go," said Uncle Tony. "Do I need to talk to your parents about you being out this late at night?"

"Oh no," said Jen. "We don't need to bother them. I just lost track of time; I promise it won't happen again."

"Well, Ok," said Uncle Tony. "Have a good night."

Jen stood on her front porch, motionless, wondering what her parents would think. She knew she wasn't even supposed to be awake at this hour. But what would happen to Alice and Jax?

The front door opened. Jen's mom had heard something suspicious outside and was investigating. She was surprised to see Jen standing there.

"JENNIFER MAY LEVANDOVSKI! YOU KNOW BETTER THAN TO SNEAK OUT!"

Jen's mom pulled her into the doorway. "Get inside."

Jen hung her head, afraid to look at her mom, and slinked into the house. "Sorry. Alice needed me to help her with some homework. I lost track of the time."

"I'm sure that's what happened. You should have called. I don't like the idea of you walking alone late at night."

"I'm sorry."

"Why do you think we let you have a cellphone?!" Jen's mom pulled her through the living room and to the stairs. "You better be sorry. Get up to your room."

"I said I'm sorry."

"You get right to bed."

Jen trudged up the staircase towards her room.

"And what are you wearing?" her mother called after her.

"We were just playing," responded Jen.

Jen sprawled across her bed. She didn't bother to change her clothes; she buried her face into her pillow and sobbed. What happened to Jax and Alice? They were running through the woods after her, then they were gone. They just disappeared. Now where were they? Uncle Tony took the time machine. Did he take their time machine? Were they stuck there now? She'd just have to wait till morning and hope they were back in their home. There's no way she'd be able to sneak out again tonight.

Jen was up, ate breakfast, and was out the door as early as she possibly could without getting into trouble again. She ran out of her house and across the lawn to Jax and Alice's home, praying they'd be there. She sprinted up their front stairs and knocked on the door (a little harder than was really polite, but she wasn't thinking about being polite at the moment). Then she saw the doorbell and rang it a couple times too.

She waited impatiently, then rang again. Then knocked again, even harder.

The door opened. There was Mr. Whitmer. "Hello, what is it?"

"Are Jax and Alice home?"

"They are still in bed. Sleeping late, I guess."

"Are you sure? Have you seen them?" said Jen, clearly agitated.

"Is something wrong?"

"Have you seen them?"

"Not yet. What time is it?" Mr. Whitmer checked his cellphone. "Boy, you're early…"

"Can you please wake them? Uh, I, uh, we have some homework due today that we need to get finished before school."

"Ok, I guess I should wake them up anyways. I don't want them to be late for school." Mr. Whitmer paused for a moment, thinking. "You want to wait in the kitchen? You can work on your homework there."

Jen pushed past Mr. Whitmer, and dropped her bag on the kitchen table.

Mr. Whitmer watched her. Something must be wrong, he thought. Then he turned and walked up the stairs to the kids' rooms.

He came to Jax's room first. He knocked on the door: no answer. He knocked again. He slowly opened the door. "Jax, you in here?" Jax was sleeping in his bed.

"Jax," his dad called out.

Jax didn't wake up. His dad started walking towards the bed. "Jax, wake up. It's time to get up. Jax, you're going to be late."

Jax didn't move.

"Jax! I'm not joking. Jax?" Mr. Whitmer reached down to grasp Jax's shoulder and give him a little shake. But it wasn't Jax in the bed. It was some pillows with the blanket pulled up over them, and a mop for hair. Jax's dad pulled back the blanket. "Jax?!"

Mr. Whitmer hurried over to Alice's room. He didn't bother to knock. Alice was in her bed. Was that really her? He pulled back the covers, and again it was just some pillows and a mop.

What was going on? "Jax! Alice!" he yelled. "WHERE ARE YOU! This is not a funny joke! COME OUT NOW!"

Jen could hear Mr. Whitmer yell, and she heard him stomp hurriedly back down the stairs.

She got up from the table and began to walk towards the living room.

Mr. Whitmer rushed into the kitchen, and nearly ran into her.

He dropped to his knees and grabbed her by the shoulders. "Do you know where they are?" he asked.

"I don't know," she said.

"You know something, you were worried, you knew something was wrong."

"I don't know where they are. I swear"

Mr. Whitmer gave Jen a very stern look. "You're not going to be in trouble. Where do you think they might be? I need to know."

"You won't believe me."

"Tell me."

Jen could tell him about the time machine, but he would never ever believe her. Or she could say they needed to talk to Uncle Tony, but she knew that adults would usually get really stubborn when they thought you were lying to them or even just making something up, and they'd refuse to ask another adult if it was true because they wouldn't want to look stupid. So Jen sat and thought for a moment, trying to figure out how to get Mr. Whitmer to talk to Uncle Tony without mentioning the time machine—that is, until she had a chance to confront Uncle Tony about the time machine in front of Mr. Whitmer.

"I think they are in Uncle Tony's lab, at school."

"Why would they be there?"

The Forbidden Treasure

"They wanted to do some experiments and they didn't think Uncle Tony would let them use his equipment."

"And you think they would have been there all night?"

Jen nodded. "They must have got locked in. We need to get Uncle Tony to let us in."

~ Chapter 11 ~

The Confrontation

Uncle Tony's front door was half open. Mr. Whitmer rang the doorbell. "Tony? Are you in there?" Mr. Whitmer pushed the door open and entered the house. "Tony?"

They found Uncle Tony on the floor of his office. The office was torn apart, books strewn all over the floor, a desk lamp shattered. His safe was open, and empty. Mr. Whitmer rushed over to him.

"Tony! Wake up," said Mr. Whitmer.

Tony woke, groggy and confused. "What?"

"Are you ok? Why are you lying on your floor?" asked Mr. Whitmer.

Uncle Tony sat up. "I... I don't know." In a daze he looked around the room. Then suddenly—remembering what had happened—his gaze darted at the safe. "Where's my gold?"

"Your gold?" replied Mr. Whitmer. "What gold?"

"What, oh, nothing," said Uncle Tony, "I meant, uh, I mean... " he trailed off slowly, not finishing his sentence.

"Where is Jax and Alice?" demanded Jen.

"What? I don't know," said Uncle Tony.

"Jen said she thought they tried to get into your lab last night," said Mr. Whitmer.

"In my lab? No, they aren't."

"Yes, they are," said Jen. "We need to go to your lab."

"No!" Uncle Tony said defensively. He took a deep breath to calm himself. He continued, "They can't be."

Mr. Whitmer was suspicious. "How can you be sure? It wouldn't hurt to check."

"But, how would they have gotten in?"

"We stole a key," said Jen.

The grownups stared at her in amazement.

"I'm sorry," she said. "I know we shouldn't have. We weren't trying to be bad, we were just playing, just needing supplies for our Detective Club. We didn't mean to do anything bad."

Uncle Tony was right where Jen wanted him to be. He'd have to take Mr. Whitmer to the lab.

"I know they're in your lab," said Jen.

"You said you didn't know where they were," said Mr. Whitmer.

Oops, she may have gone a bit too far. "I mean, since they weren't at home, and they said they were going to the lab last night, I'm certain that's where they'll be."

"We'll start there then," said Mr. Whitmer. "Ok, Tony?"

Uncle Tony did not want to take his brother to his lab, but he knew there wasn't any way to get out of it without making him even more suspicious. So he'd let them in quickly, look around, and then get them out of there. He wasn't exactly sure of what was going on, but he was sure he didn't want them in his lab.

Uncle Tony unlocked the door to his lab and pushed it open. He stepped a little way in, but not far enough for Mr. Whitmer to get by him without pushing him. "Jax? Alice?" he called out. "You in here?"

"Jax? Alice?" Mr. Whitmer called out behind Uncle Tony. "This is your dad. If you are in there, come out now."

"Well, just like I thought. They aren't here."

Jen pushed past Uncle Tony. "Hey!" He tried to grab her, but she slipped free and ran towards the back corner where the time machine was. "Careful, you'll break something!" He hurried after her.

Mr. Whitmer followed closely behind.

Jen sprinted straight for the time machine and yanked the tarp off.

"Don't touch that!" bellowed Uncle Tony.

"It's a time machine Mr. Whitmer I know it sounds crazy but it's true that it's a time machine and Alice Jax Katie Mason and I have all gone back in time with it and me Jax and Alice went back in time with it last night and I don't know what happened to them but he found me and took me back to our time and I think Jax and Alice are stuck in the past…"

"Why didn't you tell me they were with you last night!?" Uncle Tony exclaimed, "You let me leave them there."

"What is she talking about?" asked Mr. Whitmer. "What is going on?"

"You just have to believe me, Mr. Whitmer. It's a time machine, I swear."

"Jen, I've had enough of your fooling around," said Mr. Whitmer. "I'm worried about Alice and Jax, and you need to tell me the truth."

"I am!" She stomped her foot.

"You don't really expect me to believe this is a time machine. You're nine years old. Tell me the truth: where are they?"

"She is telling you the truth," said Uncle Tony.

Mr. Whitmer turned to face his brother, and took a deep breath. "Tony, come on." He gently placed a hand on Tony's shoulder. "This is why we moved here, to help you. Don't tell me you're having another breakdown."

"I'll prove it." said Tony.

* * * *

"It should be right over there," said Jax and pointed towards where the time machine had been.

Alice pointed the flashlight, but there was no time machine, just a large indent in the ground, which they both knew meant the time machine had been there and now was gone.

There was a sizzling sound, and their ears began to hurt, and then a flash of light blinded them, and a shockwave knocked them over.

When their eyes readjusted and they could see again, Alice pointed the flashlight back at where a moment ago the time machine hadn't been, and there it was.

Someone was stepping out, but they also had a flashlight and were pointing it back at Jax and Alice, so they couldn't make out who it was.

"Jax? Alice?" Uncle Tony called out. "Is that you?"

Now the thing about time travel is, though it took half a day for Jen to tell Uncle Tony that Jax and Alice had gotten left back in time—which wouldn't have taken as long if she had just told him to start with, but she didn't trust him, and thought she had to trick him into it—Uncle Tony was able to come back to just after the moment he and Jen had left, what was for them the night before. (But it was really a night about 150 years ago—this can all be really confusing.)

They wouldn't want to go back to the exact same time, because then there would be two Uncle Tonys and two Jens at the same moment, and that could cause problems. You never know what would happen with the fabric of reality, or your own state of mind, in that sort of situation.

"It's ok," Uncle Tony said. "It's me, Uncle Tony. Jen told me you were here. I never would have left you on purpose." Uncle Tony approached them cautiously, his hands out to assure them he wasn't going to hurt them. "I'm here to help you. You don't need to be afraid of me. You're not in trouble. I would never hurt you."

Alice began to cry. She had never really considered the idea that she could be left back in another time period. And now that she realized it almost happened, she was overwhelmed by the fear that it almost happened, and the relief it didn't.

"It's alright," said Uncle Tony. "I've got you; you're safe now."

Willard

~ Chapter 12 ~

What Now?

Jax and Alice sat in their living room on an old brown leather couch, looking down at their feet; Jax's ankle was in a cast. Their dad sat beside them. Uncle Tony sat in an armchair near the window, his face buried in his hands.

Their mom stood in the middle of the room, her hands on her hips. She'd been talking very sternly to them for about fifteen minutes. She hadn't let them say much of anything. She wasn't interested in their side of the story.

"Alice and Jax, you are almost ten, I expect you to behave better than this, and you clearly showed me that you cannot handle responsibility, and furthermore, I have told you multiple times *not* to mess with your father's tools. And I absolutely should never have to tell you to not break into anyone's house, or their lab, or to not use machines that you have no idea how to use, or what could happen if you use them. You will be grounded, and if you fool around with anything of your uncle's ever again, you will be severely punished. I don't know what I'll do, but you won't like it, I promise you."

"But, mom," Jax protested, "are we just supposed to forget that Uncle Tony has a time machine?"

"That's none of your business," their mom replied. "Now go to your room."

Alice began, "Mom…"

Their mom interrupted, "I don't want to hear it."

"We don't need to hear another word," said their dad. "You understand, you could have died."

"Dad, let us talk," Alice said.

"I've heard enough," their dad said. "We've heard you. It's over."

"Daaad!"

"NO, ALICE! I can't believe you kids acted so foolishly!"

"You're rude," Alice objected.

"Go upstairs!" their dad said angrily.

Jax sat next to Alice on her bed. "But where did it go?" he said.

"I don't know," said Alice.

"Uncle Tony found us, and we came back here. The moment we got back home and I had a chance to check the bag, the amulet was gone."

"Did Uncle Tony take it?"

"I don't know how he could have. I had the bag the whole time he was helping you walk."

"So it just disappeared?"

Alice shrugged. "I don't know what could have happened to it."

"Uncle Tony must have gotten it somehow."

"I don't think so. He's not acting all weird like before. And Jen said when her and dad found him all the gold was gone out of his safe. So I think we stopped him from finding the amulet and from ever getting the gold. We must have."

Jax sighed. "I'll feel a lot better when we know for sure that it's destroyed."

Alice threw herself back on her bed. "I know, but it worked. Somehow, we changed things."

"For now," said Jax.

"We have to destroy it," said Mrs. Whitmer.

"I can't," said Tony. "There's so much we can do with it."

"It's too dangerous, Tony," said Mr. Whitmer. "You know that. Our kids nearly got stuck in the old west, and could have died."

Tony pleaded with his brother and sister-in-law. "Luke, Mary, please. Please don't destroy it. I never would have let them use it if I'd known. You know I love them. I'd never hurt them."

"We know," said Luke. "But you know what can happen when you lose control."

"You have a time machine in a high school lab," said Mary. "What did you think would happen? You can't keep something like that safe."

"It's my life's work," said Tony. "I'm not meant to just be a high school science teacher. You know that. Mary, you get to do meaningful work at the university. You should understand. This will change my life. I can be a real scientist again."

"You can't put children's lives in danger," said Mary.

"I didn't mean to." Tony stood up and took Mary's hands in his. He looked her in the eyes. "I could win the Nobel Prize," he pleaded.

"You could end up dead," said Luke. "As soon as people find out about this, all the worst criminals and corrupt politicians will want it to make themselves rich. They'll steal it, and they'll kill you."

"But think of all the good things we could do with it," said Tony.

"Then why haven't you?" asked Luke.

Tony didn't answer.

Luke continued, "What have you been doing with it?"

Tony flopped back down in the armchair. "I don't quite remember, really."

Mary and Luke waited. Tony was looking out the window, thinking.

"It only takes you through time. Whatever place you start in, that's where you end up. When I travel through time, I'm still here in Mystery Lake, or the place that will become Mystery Lake. I haven't tried to go forward, so I don't know what will happen then. But I can't go back very far before I'm stuck in a wilderness. I was trying to learn about the native peoples who lived in this area, and the settlers who built this town."

"Is that where you got the gold?" asked Luke.

"That's what I can't quite remember. I must have been doing some prospecting, but it's all a bit of a blur, like a dream I can't remember. But there was something else, something bad, a nightmare. I don't know what it was."

"That's why we have to destroy the machine," said Mary.

"I know," said Tony.

"I'm sorry," said Mary. "You are a great scientist. I know that. Others will see that too someday." Mary sighed. "I'm sure I'd be able to help you get a job at the university."

* * * *

Two months passed. The adults refused to talk to the kids about the time machine anymore. The kids eventually gave up asking.

With the new friends they had made, the twins settled into the school without much trouble. Zach still tried to bother Jax every now and again. But with the help of his friends, and his sister, Jax was able to get Zach to leave him alone most of the time, and avoid him when he needed to.

The Detective Club went back to working on less dangerous mysteries. They helped their neighbors find lost cats, found a home for a stray dog, recovered a stolen bike, and other things like that.

Uncle Tony was friendly, and took them on hikes, and to the movies. But they were still a little afraid of him. Tony could tell that he made them a bit nervous, which made him sad. So he tried a little extra to be the cool uncle. Jax and Alice knew he was trying, so they tried not to be too shy when he asked them about what they were up to.

Jax and Alice still looked for the amulet whenever they had a chance. They had searched everywhere they could possibly think of and couldn't even find a clue. Alice would sit up late at night, racking her brain, trying to figure out how she could have lost it—where it might have fallen out—but nothing.

On a cold November Saturday morning, Alice was sitting in her bedroom, looking out the bay window towards the McQueen Manor. Could the amulet still be in there somewhere? Had she dropped it that night? Did Alistair find it and take it with him?

Whatever happened, the history books still showed he lost his money and left town in disgrace, unable to pay a mountain of debts. That train still got blown up. And they never did find anything to prove their uncle was Alistair's assistant.

As Alice tried to think of some place they might not have looked, or some different ideas of what might have happened, she absent-mindedly ran her fingers over the window trim. Her fingers found that old loose seam in the paneling.

She stopped, realizing what her fingers had found. She looked down at the paneling. *Oh, this,* she thought. *How did I forget about this?*

I guess a lot had happened back then that made her forget. She pulled at the loose piece, pulling open the little secret compartment.

She peered into the hole. It was so dark in there, she couldn't see a thing. Alice ran downstairs and grabbed a flashlight.

Willard

She shone the light into the secret hiding place. (Can you guess what she found?)

The Forbidden Treasure

~ Chapter 13 ~

Things Do Not Go as Planned

They had found the amulet. The thing they had searched for all-over had been in the secret hiding place in Alice's room all this time. Now what? How would they destroy it?

The amulet sat in the middle of the basement floor in the old McQueen Manor, candlelight glinting off it.

A meeting of the Detective Club was in session. They sat in a circle around it.

"We could smash it with a hammer," said Mason.

"Do you think that could work?" asked Katie.

"My dad has a really big sledge hammer," Mason responded.

"Oh!" Jax was excited. He had a really good idea. "We could put it in the time machine and send it way back in time."

"But then we really wouldn't know it was destroyed, just gone, and whatever is in that thing could still hurt people," said Alice.

"If we send it back about 4.5 billion years, we can be pretty sure it will be destroyed," said Jax.

Alice considered this. "Well, yeah. But we don't know where the time machine is anymore. And we did hear mom tell Uncle Tony to destroy it."

"Yeah," said Jax, "that is a problem."

"How did it end up in your room?" asked Jen.

"I don't know," said Alice.

"So was it there all the time?" Jen continued.

"I don't want to think about it," Alice said. "I just want to get rid of it.

Luckily for Alice, the amulet hadn't started talking to her yet. But she didn't want to keep it around long enough for that to start up again. Besides, she couldn't be sure it wasn't talking to one of the other kids and she just couldn't hear it, same way Jax didn't hear it when it spoke to her. Either way, it creeped her out.

The thing had a feeling of evil around it, and she wanted as far away from it as she could get. And she wouldn't really feel safe until she saw it destroyed.

"We could drop it in molten lava," said Mason.

"Where are we going to find that?" asked Jen, unenthusiastically.

"I don't know," said Mason. "It's just an idea."

"We could find a blacksmith. They have forges that can melt metal," said Jax. "That would probably do it. And before you ask where we are going to find one, there has to be someone around here that's into blacksmithing."

"I saw one at Fort Vancouver," said Mason. "But that's probably too far away." "Where's that?" asked Alice.

"Up by Portland," Mason replied. "Couple hundred miles away, I'd guess."

"I'd say that's too far away," said Jen.

"I saw a blacksmith at the kids' festival," said Katie.

"We can look them up on the internet," said Jax.

"Well, even if there is a blacksmith working at the children's festival, how are we supposed to convince our parents to take us there? Jacksonville is like two whole hours away. And isn't the children's festival over?" Alice asked.

"I meant the children's festival in Eugene," said Katie.

"Oh," said Alice, a little embarrassed. "My parents made us stop by Jacksonville on the way up. They said it was a cool old west town. And there was a children's festival going on. I didn't know it was a thing Oregon people did all over; I thought it was just there."

"Well, anyway," said Jen, "it is over, but that means there must be a blacksmith in the area."

Mason pulled out his cellphone. "I can search the internet for one." Mason used the voice search. "Are there any blacksmiths working in Mystery Lake?" The search pulled up a page full of different blacksmiths nearby. "Wow," said Mason, "there's a bunch."

"But are they going to actually let us drop an obviously old and expensive piece of jewelry in their forge?" said Jen. "It's a good idea, but they probably would just call our parents. And then our parents would take the amulet, and one of them would go crazy like your Uncle Tony."

"I have an idea," said Mason.

As mentioned earlier, you can learn a lot from YouTube—well, that is, from those people who post very helpful videos on it, but every once in a while you have to branch out to more traditional programming. The idea that had struck Mason was that they could build their own furnace.

With just a little searching, he managed to figure out where he had seen it done and explained: on a show called James May's Man Lab. They watched the clip a couple times. They made a list of everything needed, then divided up the list, deciding who could get what, assigning everyone a job.

The Detective Club adjourned and each member set out on their own mission. They bought a metal bucket from the local hardware store, dug up some clay and sand at the lake, and borrowed a blowtorch from Mason's dad, and hair dryer from Katie's mother (without them knowing). It took a couple days, but early Saturday morning they had constructed their very own furnace.

Hidden away in the backyard of the McQueen mansion, they began their work. They set a small fire ablaze inside the furnace. Slowly feeding it with small pieces of wood and stoking it with the hair dryer, they soon had a little inferno. Once the temperature had reached, they hoped, 900 degrees—which, according to the James May show, the furnace could reach—they prepared to drop the amulet in.

Jax pulled on heavy leather gloves that went past his elbows, and covered his face with a face-shield. He picked up a long pair of thick metal tongs.

Alice opened up a small wooden box which held the amulet.

Jax reached into the box with the tongs and grasped the amulet.

"STOP!" the thing in the amulet screeched.

Jax hesitated, his face drained of color.

"Did you hear that!?" asked Alice, her voice trembling.

Jax nodded his head.

"What was that?" asked Jen, her eyes wide with fear.

"I heard it too," said Katie. She began to back away, and prepared herself to run.

"Me too," said Mason.

"You fools!" the thing spoke with a low rasping voice that crawled up the back of your neck and burrowed its way into your skull. "I can give you whatever you want."

"Don't listen to it," said Alice. "That's the thing in the amulet. It will make us crazy if we believe it."

"Throw it in the furnace, Jax!" yelled Jen.

"NOW!" said Alice.

"NO!" the thing screamed.

Jax didn't wait a moment longer. He swiftly turned and dropped the amulet into the furnace.

Nothing happened, at least nothing they could see.

Inside the furnace the gold quickly melted away, and tiny little fissures began to splinter through the emerald.

The children waited, holding their breaths.

And then there was a slight high-pitched whistle. It startled softly, then grew in volume until it became a shrill, ear-piercing screech. The children staggered back from the furnace covering their ears. The glass in the mansion's near-by windows cracked, popped, and shattered.

"GET AWAY FROM IT!" Alice shouted as loud as she possibly could.

Alice sprawled face first onto the ground. It was just in time—the furnace exploded in a ball of flame.

The explosion knocked all the kids to the ground.

There was a quiet moment of fear – but yes, they were all alive.

They dusted themselves off; checked their wounds – nothing serious. Other than some small scrapes and cuts, and some singed hair, they were unharmed.

Then Alice heard a maniacal laugh—like it was right in her brain. She pushed herself up off of her stomach and spun around to look at the place the furnace had been. There was nothing but a black crater. But still she heard the laugh. "Jax, do you hear that?"

"Hear what?" asked Jax. "I can hardly hear a thing."

"Do you hear that laughing?" asked Alice. "Do any of you hear that horrible evil laugh?"

"No," said Jax.

Alice looked at Mason and Katie—they shook their heads.

Jen pushed herself up to her knees. "I don't hear it either." She rubbed her ears. "Is it that thing?"

"Maybe it's just my imagination," said Alice.

"Oh, Alice," said the voice in her head. "Thank you. You've set me free."

"No," whispered Alice. "No!"

"What is it?" asked Jax.

"I don't think that worked," said Alice.

Jax got up and went to inspect the remains of their furnace. "It's destroyed. There's little pieces of the emerald here. It's all broken up."

"Pick all the pieces up," said Jen. "We'll drop them in the middle of the lake. Nobody will find them there."

The next Monday, they all gathered for lunch in the cafeteria. They weren't in a talkative mood. They just sat at the table, lunches spread out in front of them, hardly eating.

Finally, Mason said, "I'm grounded for a month."

"Did they believe it was just an experiment we were doing at our Detective Club?" asked Jen.

"Yeah," said Mason. "But my dad was still mad I took his blowtorch. He tried to tell me I couldn't play with you guys at all anymore, but my mom wouldn't allow it. She said it was good for me."

"I don't think the Detective Club experiment excuse is much of an excuse anymore," said Jax.

"I didn't tell my mom what happened to her hair dryer," said Katie. "She blamed my sister for taking it.

The Forbidden Treasure

My sister is always so worried about her hair, my mom didn't suspect me."

"Did anyone hear whatever that thing was talking to them after we blew it up?" asked Jen.

No one responded.

"Alice?" Jen asked.

"No," Alice said. "It must be gone. After that explosion, my ears were ringing." She rubbed the back of her head. "My parents took me to the hospital. They said I had a concussion."

"I was fine," said Jax. "But Alice hit her head really hard when she fell."

"I think it was just my imagination," said Alice. "I was just so scared. But I'm fine now; I'm sure it's gone." She took a bite of PB&J.

"It's going to be really hard finding a mystery to rival that adventure," said Jen. "I don't know what we're going to do the rest of the year."

"That was enough adventure for me for a long time," said Alice.

* * * *

But unfortunately for Alice, Jax, Jen, Katie, Mason, and the rest of the citizens of Mystery Lake, more hair-raising adventures were in their future.

THE END (For Now)

The Forbidden Treasure

Willard

Historical Note

In the initial preparation phase of this book, we had planned for the children to encounter the native people who lived in Oregon before foreign settlers moved into the area. And in another trip through time to encounter and help Kintpuash (aka Captain Jack), and the Modoc tribe resist their forced return to the reservation.

But as we began to research, we decided it could be disrespectful to incorporate their history into this particular story as planned.

Native people have been mistreated throughout the Americas in many different ways, and the indigenous people of Oregon have their own horrific story to tell. There are many stories that should be told. Perhaps we can do that properly in a future book.

For this book we simply wanted to acknowledge the terrible way in which they were treated, but didn't feel able to do more. We have tried to accurately capture how settlers viewed and treated the native people. Yet the event in this book is not a description of one particular historical event.

The people who inhabited the land where we live in Southern Oregon are called the Takelma. We encourage you to learn more about the people who lived in your area before you, and their history.

Willard

The Forbidden Treasure

About the Authors

This is the first book written and illustrated by the Willards – Nathan (dad), Cosette (daughter, age 11), and Cillian (son, age 9).

They live in Southern Oregon with Jessi (wife and mother), and three cats – Doom, Mittens, and Boo.

They enjoy drawing, and making up stories of imaginary creatures and places. They also enjoy getting out in the wonderful natural world around them – at least Nathan does; Cillian and Cosette usually complain at first, but they enjoy it once they get there.

To learn how they conceived of, developed, and wrote this story together – a process that took over two years – you can see videos documenting their process on their Facebook page.

There's even a Jake and Alice Adventure short film they made (that was before they decided to change Jake's name to Jax).

Follow *Coco and Cillian's Adventures*, and see new projects as they work on them.

We'd also love to see your drawings of Alice and Jax

Go to - facebook.com/cocoandcillian

And - mysterylakeadventure.com

Made in the USA
Monee, IL
25 February 2022